PRIVATE

A NOVEL BY

KATE BRIAN

SIMON & SCHUSTER BOOKS FOR YOUNG READERS

New York   London   Toronto   Sydney

This book is a work of fiction. Any references to historical events,
real people, or real locales are used fictitiously. Other names, characters,
places, and incidents are the product of the author's imagination,
and any resemblance to actual events or locales or persons,
living or dead, is entirely coincidental.

SIMON & SCHUSTER BOOKS FOR YOUNG READERS
An imprint of Simon & Schuster Children's Publishing Division
1230 Avenue of the Americas, New York, NY 10020

Copyright © 2006 by Alloy Entertainment and Kieran Viola
All rights reserved, including the right of reproduction
in whole or in part in any form.

SIMON & SCHUSTER BOOKS FOR YOUNG READERS
and colophon are registered trademarks of
Simon & Schuster, Inc.

Produced by Alloy Entertainment
151 West 26th Street, New York, NY 10001

Cover design by Julian Peploe
Book design by Amy Trombat
The text of this book was set in Filosofia.

Manufactured in the United States of America
First Simon Pulse edition July 2006

14 16 18 20 19 17 15 13

Library of Congress Control Number 2006922004

ISBN-13: 978-1-4169-1873-8
ISBN-10: 1-4169-1873-6

WHERE BEAUTY LIVES

Where I come from everything is gray. The bland, square strip malls. The water in the lake at the center of town. Even the sunlight has a murky quality. We barely get spring and we never get autumn. The leaves fall off the sickly trees early each September before they even have a chance to change, tumbling down on the shingled roofs of the standard-issue houses, each one exactly the same as the last.

If you want to see beauty in Croton, Pennsylvania, you've got to sit in your ten-by-ten bedroom in your boring split-level house and close your eyes. You have to use your imagination. Some girls see themselves walking red carpets with movie-star boyfriends while flashbulbs pop. Others, I'm sure, go the princess route, conjuring up diamonds and tiaras and knights on white horses. All I imagined my entire ninth grade year was this:

Easton Academy.

How I found myself there, in the place of my daydreams, while the rest of my classmates were entering the dank dreariness of Croton High, I still am not totally sure. Something to do with my soccer and lacrosse skills, my grades, the stellar recommendation of outgoing Easton senior Felicia Reynolds (my brother Scott's older, cooler ex), and I think a little bit of begging on my father's part. But at this point, I didn't care. I was there, and this place was everything I had dreamed it would be.

As my dad drove our dented Subaru through the sunny streets of Easton, Connecticut, it was all I could do to keep from pressing my nose to the dog-slobbered window. The shops here had colorful cloth awnings and windows that gleamed. The streetlamps were the old-fashioned kind that were electric now, but had once been lit by a guy on a horse toting a pole and a flame. Potted plants hung from these lamps, bursting with bright red flowers, still dripping from a recent dousing with a garden hose.

Even the sidewalks were pretty: neat and lined with brick, topped by towering oak trees. Beneath the shade of these trees, a pair of girls my age chatted their way out of a boutique called Sweet Nothings, swinging clear bags stacked with neatly folded sweaters and skirts. As out of place as I felt in my worn Lee jeans and my blue T-shirt, I had never wanted to live anywhere more than I wanted to live here, in Easton. I couldn't believe that very soon I actually would. I felt something warm inside my chest. Something I had felt less and less over the last few years since my mother's accident. I recognized it dimly as hope.

Easton Academy is accessible by a small two-lane road, which winds up from town into the hills above. A small wooden sign on a short stone base marks the entrance to the school. EASTON ACADEMY ESTABLISHED 1858 it reads in faded letters. The sign is obscured by the low branch of a birch tree, as if to convey that if you belong here, you know where you are going, and if you do not, they aren't going to great lengths to help you find your way.

My father turned the car under the iron and brick archway and I was sucked in. Hard. Here were buildings of brick and stone, topped by shingled roofs and spires, tradition and pride oozing from every dated cornerstone. Here were ancient, weathered, arched doorways, thick wooden doors on iron hinges, cobblestone walks lined by neat beds of flowers. Here were pristine playing fields of bright green grass and gleaming white lines. Everything I saw was perfect. Nothing reminded me of home.

"Reed, you're the navigator. Where do I go?" my father asked.

Easton's orientation map had become a sweaty, crumpled ball in my hand. I flattened it over my thigh as if I hadn't memorized it ten times over. "Make a right by the fountain," I told him, trying to sound much calmer than I felt. "The sophomore girls' dorm is the last one on the circle."

We drove by a matching set of convertible Mercedes. A girl with blond hair stood idly by while a man—her father? her butler?—unloaded a huge set of Louis Vuitton luggage onto the curb. My dad whistled.

"These people sure know how to live," he said, and I was instantly irritated by his awe, even though I felt it myself. He ducked his head so he could see up to the top of the clock tower, which I knew from my many hours of paging through the Easton catalog marked the ancient library.

What I wanted to say was *"Da-a-ad!"* What I said was "I know."

He would be gone soon, and if I snapped at him I would regret it later when I was alone in this strange, picture-book place. Besides, I had a feeling that girls like the one we had just seen never said things like *"Da-a-ad!"*

Outside the three imposing dorms that stood around the circle at the midpoint of the hill, families kissed and hugged and checked that everyone had everything they needed. Boys in khakis and white shirts kicked arround a soccer ball, their blazers tossed aside, their cheeks blotched and ruddy. A pair of stern-looking teachers stood near the dry stone fountain, nodding as they spoke toward each other's ears. Girls with shimmering hair compared schedules, laughing and pointing and whispering behind their hands.

I stared at the girls, wondering if by tomorrow I would know them. Wondering if any of them would be my friends. I had never had many girlfriends. Or any, actually. I was a loner by necessity— keeping people away from my house and my mother and therefore myself. Plus there was the fact that I wasn't interested in the things most girls seemed to be interested in—clothes and gossip and *Us Weekly*.

Back home I was always more comfortable around guys. Guys didn't feel the need to ask questions, to check out your room and your house and know all the intimate details of your life. So I mostly hung out with Scott and his friends, especially Adam Robinson, whom I had dated all summer and who would be a senior at Croton High this year. I guess the fact that I had broken up with him and come here, thereby *not* being the first sophomore girl ever to have a senior boyfriend driving her to school on the first day, would be just another thing that would mystify the girls in my grade.

Of course, they were easily mystified.

I hoped it would be different here. I *knew* it would be. Look at it. How could it not be?

My dad brought the car to a stop at the curb between a gold Land Rover and a black limousine. I stared up at the ivy-covered walls of Bradwell, the sophomore dorm that would be my home for the next year. Some of the windows were already open, raining down music on the students and parents. Pink curtains hung in one room and inside a girl with jet-black curls moved back and forth, placing things, making it hers.

"Well, here we are," my dad said. There was a pause. "You sure about this, kiddo?"

Suddenly, I couldn't breathe. In all the months that my parents had argued about my coming to Easton, my father was the only person in my entire family who had never expressed a moment of doubt. Even Scott, whose idea it had been for me to follow Felicia here in the first place—she had come for her junior and senior years, finishing up last spring before heading off to Dartmouth and, undoubtedly, glory—had balked when he saw the tremendous tuition. But my dad had been on board fully from day one. He had sent in my lacrosse and soccer tapes. He had spent hours on the phone with the financial aid department. And all the while he had constantly reassured me that I was going to "knock 'em dead."

I looked into my dad's eyes, exactly the same blue as my own, and I knew he didn't doubt whether I could make it here. He doubted whether *he* could make it back home. Images of pill vials flashed in my mind. Little white and blue tablets spilled across a water ring stained night table. A bin full of empty liquor bottles and crumpled tissues. My mother, wiry and pale, grousing about her pain, about how everything bad happened to her and none of us cared, tearing me down, tearing Scott down, telling us all we were worthless just to make us feel as miserable as she did. Scott had already made his escape—he had packed up and gone off to Penn State last week. Now it would be just Dad and my mother in that tiny little house. The thought depressed me.

"I don't have to go here," I said, even though the very idea that he might agree with me made me physically ill. To see this place, feel what it was all about, and then have it all taken away within the span of five minutes would be painful enough to kill me, I was sure. "We can go home right now. Just say the word."

My dad's face softened into a smile. "Yeah, right," he said. "Like I would really do that. But I appreciate the offer."

I grinned sadly. "No problem."

"I love you, kiddo," he said. I already knew that. Getting me into this school and out of that hellhole was about the most obvious display of love any parent could have produced. He was pretty much my hero.

"Love you too, Dad."

And then he hugged me and I cried and before I knew it, we were saying good-bye.

INTIMIDATION

"Easton Academy is one of the top-ranked schools in the country. Which is, I assume, the reason you sought out a place here. But many students who matriculate in from public schools find it to be a . . . *difficult* adjustment. I trust, of course, that you will not be one of those students, am I right, Miss Brennan?"

My advisor, Ms. Naylor, had gray hair and jowls. Actual jowls. They shook when she spoke, and when she spoke it was mostly about how I never should have applied to Easton in the first place as I was completely out of my league and teetering on the brink of failure before I had even entered my first class.

At least that was what she implied.

"Right," I echoed, going for a confident smile. Ms. Naylor made an equally feeble attempt in return. I got the idea that she didn't smile much as a rule.

Her basement office was dark, the walls made of stone and lined by shelves full of dusty leather-bound books. It was lit only by two windows set high in the wall. Her round body wedged so perfectly between the arms of her chair that it seemed she was permanently bound there. If the musky/oniony smell in the air was any indication, it was quite possible that she never actually left the room. And that whatever she last ate within its four walls was seriously rank.

"The academic programs at Easton are extremely advanced. Most of the students in your year are taking courses that would be considered senior level by your old high school's curriculum standards," Ms. Naylor continued, looking down her nose at what I assumed were my Croton High records. "You'll need to do a lot of extra work to keep up. Are you up to the task?"

"Yeah. I hope so," I said.

She looked at me like she was confused. What did she expect me to say? "No"?

"I see you're here on partial scholarship. That's good," Ms. Naylor says. "Most of our scholarship students have a certain fire in their bellies that seems to inspire them to attain their goals."

Ms. Naylor closed her folder and leaned toward me across her desk. A shaft of light from one of the windows illuminated the distinct line between the makeup on her face and the fleshy rolls of her neck.

"We expect great things out of each and every one of our students here at Easton," she said. "I hold my own advisees to particularly high standards, so I will be keeping a close eye on you, Miss Brennan. Don't let me down."

Maybe I was just being paranoid, but somehow this demand

sounded more like a threat. There was a pause. I had the feeling I was supposed to say something. So I said, "Okay."

Her eyes narrowed. "Your schedule."

She whipped out a thin sheet of paper and held it out over the little bronze nameplate on the edge of her desk, advertising her position as guidance director. As far as I could tell, all she was trying to do was guide me, crying in submission, to the nearest airport.

I took the paper and scanned it, taking in words like "Art History," "Bonus Lab," and "French 3." How in God's name had I placed into French 3?

"Thank you," I said. I was pleased to hear that my voice was not trembling in concert with my insides.

"And, the honor code."

She handed me another piece of paper, this one thicker, more substantial, than the first. At the top corner was the Easton crest and the words "Easton Academy Code of Honor for Students." Beneath that, "Tradition, Honor, Excellence."

"Read it over and sign it," Ms. Naylor said.

I did as I was told. The honor code basically stated that I would not cheat and that I would report any classmate if I suspected him or her of cheating. If I failed to meet these standards, I would be instantly expelled. No second chances at Easton Academy. But since I had never had to cheat in my life, and couldn't fathom that anyone else who had been accepted to this school would have to, I signed it quickly and handed it back. Ms. Naylor inspected my signature.

"You should get going," she said. "House meetings begin in fifteen minutes. You don't want to make a bad impression with your house mother on your first day."

"Thank you," I said again, and stood.

"Oh, and Miss Brennan?" she said. When I looked at her again, she had twisted her face into a smile. Or a reasonable facsimile thereof. "Good luck," she said.

The "you'll need it" was implied.

Feeling nostalgic for the hopefulness I had felt back in my dad's car, I grasped the cold, brass doorknob and walked out.

INTRIGUE

My tendency to walk with my head down has had both benefits and drawbacks in the past. The major drawback was the fact that I had walked into my share of people. The benefit was that I was always finding things. Tons of coins, fallen necklaces and bracelets, secret love notes people thought they'd secured in their binders. Once I even found a wallet full of cash and when I turned it in I got a fifty-dollar reward. But I should have known that walking that way around Easton would be bad. I was halfway across the quad that backed the dorms when I heard someone shout, "Heads up!"

Which, of course, made me look when it was supposed to make me duck.

I dropped my schedule and grabbed the football out of the air about a tenth of a second before it would have sent me to the infirmary with a broken nose. My heart was in my throat.

"Nice reflexes."

There was a guy sitting directly in my path. Had the ball not almost rearranged my face, I would have tripped right over him with my next step. He slipped the sleek cell he'd been texting on into his pocket, unfolded his long legs, and stood up, picking up my schedule along the way. His dark hair fell over his forehead in a messy yet somehow totally deliberate way, one lock landing right over one of his strikingly deep blue eyes. He wore a gray heather T-shirt that hugged a perfectly lithe frame. His features were angular, his lightly tanned skin flaw-free.

"New girl," he said, looking me up and down.

I flushed. "That obvious?"

"I know everyone that goes to this school," he said.

"Everyone?" I said. Hardly possible.

"It's a small school," he said, studying me.

Didn't feel that way to me. In fact, it felt pretty damn huge. But then, it was my first day.

"Pearson! Quit flirting and throw the ball back!"

Before I had only *felt* the guys hovering. Now "Pearson" held his hand out for the ball and I looked up at his friends, six of them, all sweating and heaving for breath about twenty yards away. Rather than handing it over, I turned, took a few steps, and punted the ball to the guy farthest from me. It fell right into his hands. One of the players—a tall, broad, blond kid who had "cocky" written all over him—threw me a lascivious glance before jogging back into the game.

"Reed Brennan. Sophomore."

My heart skipped a disturbed beat. "Pearson" was reading my schedule.

"I'll take that back now," I said, reaching for it.

He turned away from my grasp, holding the schedule up with both hands. I racked my brain trying to recall if there was anything embarrassing or overly personal on there. Did it say I was on scholarship? Did it say where I was from?

"Hmmmm. . . tough schedule. We have a smarty on our hands."

The way he said it, I wasn't sure if it was a good thing or a bad thing. "Not really," I replied.

"And modest, too," he said, sliding a glance in my direction. "You're one of those girls, aren't you?"

I was flaming red by this point. "What girls?"

"Those girls who are smart but pretend they're not. Those girls who are absolutely model-level gorgeous but are always saying they're ugly," he said.

Gorgeous? *Gorgeous?* I hated compliments. Never had any idea what to do with them. Especially ones I suspected were backhanded.

"Those girls whose very existence tortures all the other self-esteem-lacking girls around her."

I snatched my schedule out of his hands and stuffed it into my back pocket.

"I guess that makes you one of those obnoxious guys who thinks he knows everything and is so full of himself that he's convinced that everyone around him wants to hear his every last unoriginal thought," I said.

He grinned. "Got me pegged."

He didn't even have the decency to *act* offended. He had that air

about him that said he knew who he was and didn't much care what
I or anyone else thought of him. I envied that.

"Reed Brennan, sophomore, I'm Thomas Pearson, senior," he
said, offering his hand.

No one even close to my age had ever offered to shake my hand
before. I eyed him uncertainly as I slipped my hand into his. His
palm was unbelievably warm and the firm assuredness of his grip
sent a rush of anticipation right through me. As he stared directly
into my eyes, his smile slowly widened. Did he feel it too, or did he
just know somehow that *I* felt it?

His cell phone rang and he finally pulled away, sliding it out of
his left pocket. Odd, I had thought he'd placed it in the other one.
"I have to take this," he said, spinning the phone on his palm like a
six-shooter in an old western. "Business before pleasure. And trust
me, it *was* a pleasure to meet you, Reed Brennan."

I opened my mouth, but nothing came out.

"Pearson," he said into the phone.

Then he strolled off, head up, so comfortable that he may as well
have owned the place. I wondered if he actually did.

HOUSING'S IDEA OF A JOKE

My roommate was a talker. Her name was Constance Talbot and she apparently lacked the need for oxygen. She started talking the moment I entered our room after my encounter with Thomas Pearson and didn't come up for air once. While she blabbed, I checked out the posters of rock bands and Rodin paintings she had hung in my absence. Took in the piles of cardigans and T-shirts and low-rise cords on her bed. Wondered if her Manhattan school had kicked her out for continuously disturbing the peace.

Her favorite topic of conversation? Herself. Making me wonder if I had been idiotic to think that the girls here would be different. In those five minutes I found out that she was an only child, that she was new to Easton like me, that she had attended a private school in Manhattan and could have kept going there but felt the need to "expand her horizons," that her dog was unfortunately named Pooky, and that she had a boyfriend back on the Upper East Side even more unfortunately named Clint.

"Clint and I went to the U2 concert last summer at the Garden.

Not like anyone *wants* to go to the Garden, but where else is U2
gonna play, right? So my dad gets us backstage passes because he
was promoting it, and—did I mention that my dad is a promoter?"

    She had.

    "And he was all like, 'The band isn't going to be back there, but
you'll get to see where they get dressed and hang out.' But then we
get back there and open the door and guess who's standing there?
Guess!"

    It was actually my turn to talk.

    "Bono?" I said.

    "Bono!" she exclaimed. "Right there! Like five feet away! And
do you know what he said? He said, and I quote, 'Pleasure to meet
you. . . .' "

    Her Irish accent was really bad.

    " 'You have some of the most gorgeous Irish skin I've ever seen.'
He knew I was Irish! Just from looking at me!"

    Apparently Bono was neither blind nor stupid. After all,
Constance had the requisite thick red hair. The freckles. The green
eyes. I wouldn't have been surprised if she had Erin Go Bragh tat-
tooed across her ass.

    Except that she was too wide-eyed and perky to be the tattoo type.

    "So of course I asked him to pose for a picture with me and of
course he did. My friend Marni took like a hundred of them—"

    "Really? Do you have them?" I asked, trying to make an effort.

    There was at least a five-second pause as Constance turned her
back on me and dug through her pink satin jewelry box—so long

that I grew concerned. "Oh, no. I didn't bring them with me. I didn't want to, you know, show off."

Right.

"Anyway!" She was back in my face, bright smile and all, fastening a beaded necklace around her neck. "Are you ready?"

"For what?"

"For the house meeting!" she said, her abnormally large eyes bulging. "We're gonna meet our house mother!"

"Oh. Right," I said, scooting forward on my plaid comforter.

"Doesn't that sound so seventeen hundreds? We have a *house mother*," Constance said, cracking herself up. "I can't wait to meet the rest of the girls on our floor."

She looked at me expectantly. "Yeah. Me neither," I said, forcing a smile.

I followed her out the door, wishing I felt half as excited and confident as she did. Unfortunately, I had already seen the girls on our floor. Seen them chatting on their cell phones, folding their two-hundred-dollar jeans, toting their Kerastase hair products into the bathroom, and I already knew that I was in over my head. And they all seemed as if they already knew one another. They approached one another easily and talked like old friends—as if they had all lived here together their entire lives, cultivating private jokes and creating a specific style that I would never be able to match, having come to the game so late. There wasn't a single item in my closet that wouldn't make me stick out like a Podunk loser—a Wal-Mart frequent shopper.

I didn't know how to do this. I didn't know how to chat and tell secrets and be friends. No classmate of mine had been inside my house since I was eight. I didn't do birthday parties or slumber parties or anything else, and as a result no one at my old school knew anything about me. Which was just the way I wanted it. I had made that choice back when my mother had first begun her long and continuous downward spiral. To protect myself. To protect other people from her. And it had worked all this time. Not a soul outside my immediate family knew my secrets.

What I had never realized was that after seven years of antisocial behavior, I had rendered myself incompetent. Incapable of teenage normalcy. I was a sorry excuse for a girl. And no matter how much I wanted to, I was starting to wonder if there was anything I could do to change. If there was anything I could possibly do to make people *want* to get close to me. Especially these people. Less than five hours at Easton and I was already fairly certain my girlfriendless drought would continue.

THEM'S THE RULES

The meeting was being held in the common room on our floor—fifth floor, Bradwell. The U-shaped hallway of our dorm terminated at each end with a door to the common room. Beyond this room were the elevators to the lobby, which meant that in order to get to your room you had to walk through the common room and take one of the two doors to your side of the building. When I had come through earlier, the well-worn couches and chairs had been placed all around the room, creating nooks for studying and one television-viewing area. Now all the seating had been arranged in a wide V, facing the TV. Dozens of girls crowded on and around the couches and chairs, chatting and laughing. The place was packed and the decibel level was staggering. A thick concoction of perfumes—and scented hair products and scented lotions—choked the air. Constance bounded right into the room and took a seat on the arm of one of the couches. The girl at the end, who now had a perfect view of Constance's ass, rolled her eyes and pulled her arm in close to herself. I hovered by the door. There seemed to be more oxygen there.

A young woman stood near the TV making notes on her clip-board. When Constance had entered, she'd looked up and smiled. Her long, smooth hair was pulled back in a plaid headband and if I bumped into her on the street I never would have pegged her for any older than seventeen. She checked her gold watch and wrinkled her nose quickly.

"Okay! It's about that time! Let's get started," she said. "Come in, come in." She waved me into the room and everyone turned around to look. With no other options in sight, I walked around to the end of the V, dropped to the floor near Constance's feet, and hoped that everyone would stop staring.

"Hello everyone, and welcome to Easton Academy. I am Ms. Ling, your house mother." She paused and laughed. "That sounds so old. Do I look old enough to be your 'mother'?" she added, throwing in a couple of air quotes, made awkward by the clipboard and pen in her hands.

A few people laughed halfheartedly. Even more rolled their eyes. Ms. Ling didn't seem to notice. She crossed her legs at the ankle and hugged the clipboard to her chest.

"A little bit about me," she said with a smile." I graduated from Easton Academy six years ago. Lived in this very dorm my freshman and sophomore years. This was back before they built the freshmen their own dorm," she added with a sly smile. She wanted us to feel like she was one of us. Or maybe *she* just wanted to feel like she was still one of us. "After I graduated, I went to Yale undergrad and Harvard grad where I received my master's degree in East Asian studies last spring. After that, I am proud to say that Easton invited me back to be the first ever teacher of Chinese language and culture. So if any of you are interested, it's a beautiful language and there's still time to transfer into the intro class."

Silence.

Ms. Ling blinked. It seemed like she had expected a few enthusiastic volunteers and our nonexistent reaction threw her. She stood up straight and cleared her throat, checking her clipboard.

"Okay, onto the rules. I know some of you have heard these before, but bear with me," Ms. Ling said. "I have to go over everything. Them's the rules."

She flushed when, once again, no one laughed. Didn't she realize that trying too hard was about the worst thing she could do if she wanted us to think she was cool? I mean, according to her autobiography she had *been* one of us only six years ago. Did people really forget that quickly?

"First, let's talk about curfew," she said, earning a few groans which actually seemed to perk her up. We were alive!

What followed was a long litany of the rules and regs, all of which were listed in the Easton Handbook we all had back in our rooms. Of course, I had thought that some of them were just for show—to make the parents feel like they were sending us to a nice, strict, no-nonsense school—but it turned out that they were all real and that the school took them very seriously. We really did have to sign in with Ms. Ling in her room on the first floor every night before ten. After that, we weren't allowed to leave our floors without express permission from Ms. Ling herself. There were quiet hours every night from six until nine and we were not allowed inside Bradwell between classes. Guys were only allowed inside the dorm between the hours of six and nine each night, and then they were only permitted in the common rooms (this announcement was met with a few snickers, the most obvious of which came from a sort of pig-faced girl with blond hair and big boobs who sat in the center of the V). Once she was done reading us the three-page-long list, Ms. Ling looked up and grinned.

"So that's it! If you have any questions, please feel free to come see me in my room. I have a really good feeling about this group. It's going to be a great year! I look forward to getting to know each and every one of you!"

She had to yell that last part because everyone was already on their feet and heading for the doors.

THE GIRL IN THE WINDOW

That night, since there was nothing to study for yet, quiet hours were suspended so that each floor could have a little get-to-know-you party. I was never good at parties, so I was kind of dreading it, even though I knew I should just go. If I wanted a new start, I was going to have to go against instinct, which meant being social. The very idea gave me cramps, though, so I avoided thinking about it and flipped through my Easton Handbook on my bed while Constance got ready. And talked.

"So when we *finally* got to the bottom of the mountain, I was totally dehydrated and had this streak of mud all the way up my side and this guide was waiting for us there and he was like, 'Did you not see the trail?' and we were like, '*What* trail?'"

I smirked because I could feel her looking at me and it sounded like the point in the story where she would expect some kind of reaction.

"Anyway, are you ready?"

The moment of truth. I put the book down. "Maybe I'll come

down later." I honestly didn't know until that moment that I wasn't going to go. But I didn't take it back.

"Want to make an entrance, huh?" she joked.

Not remotely.

"Something like that," I said.

"Okay," she said with a shrug. "But don't blame me if all the good pizza's gone!"

I'll live.

"Don't worry about it," I said.

As soon as the door was closed I felt really bad for bailing. What was wrong with me? There was no way I was ever going to make friends if I sat alone in my room. I knew this. But still, somehow, I couldn't make myself move.

I sighed and leaned back against the denim pillow my brother had bought me at Target, settling into my self-imposed exile. So this was my new home. This square, cream-colored box with its creaky wooden floor, standard issue twin beds, matching desks, and five-drawer dressers, one of which I couldn't even fill. Within five seconds of seeing my half-empty side of the huge closet, Constance had asked, "Do you mind?" and then promptly jammed up the empty space with three extra wool coats and a puffy black parka. It all contributed to my feeling that I didn't fit or, more accurately, that there wasn't enough of me to fill a place like this.

I heard laughter outside the window and stood up. The large bay window with a sill big enough to sit on was, hands down, the best feature of our room. Earlier, Constance had gone out to meet some of our floor-mates and had come back beaming, happy to report that only two rooms had a window like this and we were beyond lucky to get one. I sat down on the sill and stared out the last window pane. Another peal of laughter rang somewhere out in the darkness and my heart ached. What the hell was I doing here? How could I possibly have thought this would be a good idea?

Leaning my temple against the glass, I willed myself not to cry. This was unbelievable. Was I really homesick? For what? For my pins-and-needles home life? For the cinderblock halls of my old high school? For the *strip malls*? My mind flashed on my father and on Adam, who had never been anything but sweet to me. I saw my dog, Hershey, wagging his tail when my dad got home, expecting to see me as well. I saw the ugly flowered wallpaper my parents had hung in my bedroom before they knew I was a tomboy, wallpaper I had always hated but which now felt like the perfect emblem of home. I thought of the lacrosse team and our vow to actually get to the state championships this year. Why did all of this suddenly seem so huge? The day before I couldn't wait to get out of there.

A tear squeezed out and it was like a wake-up call. No. This was not acceptable. I was not a weakling. I had made my choice. I was not going to call my father and beg him to come back for me. There was nothing in Croton for me. Nothing worth sticking around for, anyway. I knew this. I just had to focus on it. I stared into the darkness, at the lights in the windows of the other dorms, and told myself that I belonged here. I forced myself to try to believe it.

I will be happy here. I will make friends. This is the beginning of a whole new life.

And that was when I saw her. A girl, sitting in a window just like mine, directly across the way. She was wispy and thin with delicate features, smooth pale skin, and light blond hair that fell in loose waves around her tiny shoulders. She looked almost ethereal, like she could float away at any moment with the help of a light breeze. She wore a white tank top and short pajama shorts and seemed riveted on the pages of the book she held in the crook between her bent legs and her flat stomach. I was so riveted by *her* that I didn't notice anything moving in her room until another girl swooped in out of nowhere and snatched the book out of her hands. I sat up straight, startled, thinking for a split second that the girl had been threatened. But then I saw the taller, darker girl twirl the reader into the room and onto the bed. There she joined two others who sat, laughing, their bare legs splayed out as they ate from a box of chocolates.

I turned fully toward the window now, crossing my legs Indian style in front of me and balancing precariously on the windowsill. Then the lights across the way were doused and my breath caught. Moments later, a flicker of light. Then another. Then another. Gradually the room started to glow and the figure of the dark-haired girl loomed through the dancing shadows as she lit candle after candle. Soon the four girls were bathed in the warm light. One of them rose and handed out glasses. Large, round glasses with delicate stems. Each was already filled with deep red liquid.

Wine. They were drinking wine right there in their dorm. Laughing and chatting and sipping in the candlelight.

In my entire life, I had never seen anything like these girls. They seemed so much older, and not just older than me—which they obviously were—but too old to be in high school. Every move they made was graceful and sure. The held their glasses with carefree assuredness as if they drank from such delicate crystal each and every day.

This girl, the laugher, had piled her brown hair on top of her head in a messy bun, held there by a pair of chopsticks. She was stunningly beautiful, with dark, tan skin and a lithe, athletic figure. She flashed a knowing smile, which she prefaced by a narrow, sliding glance at her friends. She wore a red silk robe over a tank top and boxers and seemed to live to tease. The second girl was petite, with messy, dark blond curls and cheeks like a porcelain doll. She was playful with the others and seemed younger than them, shoving and rolling her eyes and clapping when she laughed. But it was the reader and the dark-haired girl I couldn't tear my eyes from.

The dark-haired girl wore nothing but black underwear and a large silk nightshirt, undoubtedly made for a man, with only the two center buttons done. She shook her thick hair back, took a sip of her wine, and held the novel up to read from it to her friends, gesturing dramatically with her glass, but never spilling so much as a drop. All three of them gathered together, rapt with attention at the girl's performance, and I thought, *This girl is the leader*. As she continued to read, she placed her glass down and lifted the

ethereal girl's arm. The girl stood on cue, a slight, far-off smile playing about her lips. The dark-haired girl thrust their hands above her
head and the bottom of her shirt fell open, exposing a long, red scar
along her stomach, just above her hipbone. I was so startled by this
garish imperfection on such a flawless being that I almost looked
away. But then she stepped breast-to-breast with her friend and the
scar was covered and I realized they were dancing. They moved as
one, twirling through the shadows and the flickering candlelight. The
little cherub reached for her sound dock and acoustic guitar music
echoed through the quad, sending a shiver down my spine.

The ethereal girl spun out of her friend's arms toward the
window and suddenly she froze. My heart caught, startled at her
abruptness, but it took me a good long moment to realize she was
staring right at me. I had mistaken her gaze as flighty and unfocused, but I saw now that it was the exact opposite. She looked
right through me, around me, all over me, taking in everything and
turning me inside out. Embarrassed, I looked quickly away,
pretending to be preoccupied by something in the room, but it was
no use. I had to look back. When I did, she was holding her curtains
wide with both hands, still staring.

I was breathless. I was caught. But I couldn't look away. Would
she tell her friends? Would she report me? Could I get kicked out of
Easton for spying? I stared back, willing her to be kind. Willing her
not to tell. For a long moment, neither one of us moved.

Then she smiled, ever so slightly, and snatched the curtains
closed.

THE BILLINGS GIRLS

"Billings House? That's an upperclassmen-only house. And even if you're a junior or senior, you have to meet certain requirements to get in."

"Requirements?"

"Academic, athletic, service. If you meet their requirements, you get an invitation from housing at the end of the year. It's very selective. You have to be an integral part of the Easton community to live there."

Her expression said, "You will never live there."

I had just met Missy Thurber five minutes before and already I felt like choking her. She was the piglike girl who had snickered about the no-boys rule at yesterday's meeting. She had highlighted blond hair that she wore back in a French braid and a nose that turned up so far at the end that you could almost see into her nostrils. You'd think that a girl with a nose like that wouldn't have the guts to be so superior, but she managed to look down it at everyone she saw. She also held her shoulders so far back when she walked it

was as if she wanted her large breasts to enter any room a good fifteen seconds ahead of her. Ridiculous. I would never have even
bothered talking to her if Constance hadn't told me both her parents and all her siblings had attended Easton and that she knew
everything there was to know about the school. I had looked up the
dorm behind mine in the catalog, but other than its name, Billings,
there was no information. All the other dorms read "Bradwell,
sophomore girls' housing" or "Harden, junior and senior boys'
only." Billings just said "Billings House."

"At the end of the year, we should apply. We should *all* apply,"
Constance said in her enthusiastic way as we walked out of the
breakfast line and into the Easton cafeteria with our trays of fruit
and toast. "I bet we would totally get in," Constance added to me
alone.

The Easton cafeteria was a cavernous room with a domed ceiling
that terminated in a small, cut-glass skylight that danced slivers of
sun on the tables and chairs below. Unlike Croton High, the furni-
ture here was not made of standard-issue plastic and metal, but
real, solid wood. Cane-backed chairs were set up alongside tables
with thick legs, and all surfaces shone as if they had been freshly
waxed. On the walls were paintings that evoked various facets of life
in historical New England. Farmhouses, covered bridges, skaters
on a frozen pond. All very quaint and old-fashioned. All almost
funny when juxtaposed against the kid with the MP3 player who was
executing a sleeper hold on some other guy in an effort to comman-
deer his portable game system. Or the girls swapping summer

piercing horror stories, lifting their shirts and sticking out their tongues to display their war wounds.

Near the front of the room was a large table with slightly more ornate detailing. Several teachers sat there with their food, talking in low tones or reading from newspapers. A couple of older gentlemen sat back with their arms crossed over their chests, scanning the room as they spoke to one another, eager to pounce if someone stepped out of line.

"You don't *apply*. They invite you," Missy said again, rolling her eyes. "How did she even get in here?" she said, not so quietly, to Lorna, the mousy girl on her other side. Lorna had small features overpowered by bushy brown eyebrows and the kinkiest brown hair I had ever seen. She hadn't said much so far, but she hadn't left Missy's side all morning, so I had a feeling I didn't like her.

"Nice attitude," I said.

Missy scoffed and took a seat at the end of a table, forcing the rest of us to squeeze between her and the chair behind her to get in.

"Whatever. The point is, not just anyone can get into Billings. You have to be . . . special," Missy said as she prissily opened up her napkin and laid it across her lap.

"And it's like once you live there, you're golden," Lorna added. "They all get good grades—"

"Even if your grades sucked before. Go figure," Diana Waters, another girl from our floor, interjected. She was a pixie-ish girl with short blond hair and clear braces. "Plus every captain of every team and every president of every club lives there—"

"They're achievers," Missy said. "Women who lived in Billings have gone on to be senators, movie stars, news anchors, novelists."

"And college? Forget about it," Diana said. "They get recommendations from all the Billings alumnae and every single one of them ends up at an Ivy. Every single one."

"You're kidding," I said.

"I shit you not," Diana said. "Their track record is blemish-free."

"Yes, it is," Missy said as she spread some low-fat cream cheese on her bagel. "I can't wait until next year. To have one of those huge rooms? The cages they have us in now have *got* to be a human rights violation."

"What makes you think you're going to live there? I thought you had to be *invited*," I said pointedly.

"I will be. I'm a legacy," Missy said. Like, *duh*. "Both my mother and my sister lived in Billings."

Okay. Now I hated her even more. The fact that someone like that could just have something like Billings handed to her just illustrated everything that was wrong with the world.

"Which basically means they have to take her," Lorna added with a laugh.

Nice. Maybe Lorna didn't entirely suck.

Missy shot her a look that made her go instantly pale. "Not that you wouldn't get in anyway," Lorna added quickly.

"Check it out," Diana said, lifting her chin. "Speak of the devils."

I looked up and there they were, striding two-by-two toward a table in the very center of the cafeteria. Leading the pack was the girl with the dark hair and the scar that was now hidden somewhere underneath a pristine white linen blazer and black T-shirt. I flushed just thinking about it, knowing it was there when she had no idea that I knew. She was tall—even taller than my five nine from the looks of her—and, I couldn't help noticing, in flat shoes. She spoke to the ethereal girl, who walked next to her with her head tipped toward her friend, but with that far-off expression in her eyes.

Behind them was the sly girl, whose light brown hair was again up in a messy bun. She led with her hips as she walked, her back straight and her chin up. A gawky brunette boy stared at her as she passed him by and she winked at him surreptitiously. He turned a deep, disturbing shade of purple before sliding down in his seat and hiding behind his manga book. The girl laughed to herself, triumphant.

With her was the cherub, whose blond curls bounced as she scurried after her friends. She was the only one of the four who walked with her head down, her pale skin blotched with pink from some kind of exertion, pleasure, or embarrassment. She hugged her books to her chest and seemed to be concentrating hard on something going on in her head.

They really were here. They really did exist.

"I would kill to be Noelle Lange," Diana said, leaning her chin on her hand.

"Yeah. That's gonna happen," Missy said sarcastically.

"Which one's Noelle?" Constance asked.

"White blazer," Lorna said, envy dripping from her very lips. "Rumor has it that Harvard, Cornell, and Yale are all fighting for her."

"Please. She'll go wherever Dash McCafferty goes," Missy said, glancing over.

I saw that the big, blond guy who caught my punt yesterday was now sitting on a table behind Noelle, rubbing her shoulders with his huge hands. She tilted her head back, her long tresses tumbling down behind her, and he leaned down for a kiss.

"More like *he'll* go wherever *she* goes," Diana said. "I highly doubt Dash wears the pants in that relationship."

"When Noelle's in the room, she's pretty much the only one wearing pants," Lorna added.

"That's true. I take it back," Missy said.

"Who's the reader?" I asked, noticing that ethereal girl once again had her nose stuck in a book.

"That's Ariana Osgood," Missy said. "Her family owns half the South. Which means the rest of the Billings Girls forgive her for being *from* the South."

Diana, Constance, and Lorna all snickered.

"They're in oil," Missy added. "All big, cigar-chomping, bane-of-the-environmentalists types. God only knows how they produced her."

"She's a poet," Diana explained. "She writes half the literary magazine every quarter. She's really good."

"The model is Kiran Hayes," Lorna said. "She's done Abercrombie, Ralph Lauren . . ."

"Omigod! Yes! She was on the billboard outside my Pilates studio!" Constance exclaimed.

"Omigod! Keep your voice down, you freak!" Missy shot back, mimicking her.

"Wait. She's an *actual* model?" I asked.

"What? Like you've never seen one in the flesh before?" Missy said. "Half the girls in my building back home have done the spring shows."

I glanced around and noticed that at least half the male population of the room was in fact watching Kiran, most of them practically drooling.

"And then there's Taylor Bell," Diana said. "From all accounts, the smartest girl ever to step foot on the Easton campus."

Across the way, the cherubic girl laughed and had to slap her hand over her mouth to keep from spitting out her oatmeal. Didn't look like a genius to me, but then again, I'd never seen one of *those* in the flesh either.

"Best schools. Hottest boyfriends," Diana said. "Yeah. Being a Billings Girl definitely wouldn't suck."

I stared across the room at the four girls and the guys who hovered around them, my pulse racing with a new sense of excitement. A few more girls sat down at the other end of their table, every last one of them beautiful and poised, though to me they seemed second-string compared to the four girls I had seen the night before.

"What about the others?" I asked.

"Eh, they're in Billings too," Diana said with a wave of her fork.

So I was right. It was Noelle and her friends who were important. Noelle and her friends who were the most worth knowing.

My heart pounded against my rib cage and I pressed my sweaty palm into the thigh of my jeans. I had never wanted anything as much as I wanted to be at that table right then. If I could just enter that inner sanctum, every door at Easton would open up to me. I would never have to worry about being accepted or fitting in. I would be leaving my own crappy, depressing home life so far behind maybe I could manage to forget it altogether.

TRADITION

Easton was a nondenominational school, but it had been founded by Presbyterians back in the early nineteenth century. According to the catalog, they had discontinued group prayer in the 1990s, but they still called the morning, school-wide gathering "morning services." The daily assembly was held in the ancient chapel at the center of campus, surrounded by the class buildings, the offices of the instructors and deans, the gym, cafeteria, and library—all of which I was eager to explore. Beyond this circle were the dorms, beyond them the playing fields, and beyond them the mountains and trees and clear blue sky. It was a hot morning, normal for early September, but as we stepped through the arched doorway and into the chapel, it was like walking into a cave. Goosebumps popped out all over my skin as the cool air washed over me and I shivered in my lightweight T-shirt. Suddenly, I understood why most students had brought along cardigans or jackets. The high walls were made of cold, musty gray stone and the slim stained-glass windows only allowed the most minor shafts of sunlight to enter.

I hugged myself as I passed by the Billings Girls. Ariana was in the very last pew, reading, while Kiran and Taylor sat near the center of the chapel—Kiran studying her face in a compact mirror, Taylor scribbling in a notebook. Noelle was nowhere to be seen. It was odd, seeing them separated like this. I felt as if they were one entity and should always be by one another's sides. I took my seat with my dorm-mates near the center of the pews.

"We sit according to class. Boys on the left, girls on the right," Diana explained as we settled in. Her roommate, a girl named Kiki who could have been Diana's longer-haired twin, but wasn't, sat down next to her. I had yet to see Kiki without her iPod. She kept time to the music with her chin as she slumped down in her seat. "Up there are the frosh, behind us are the juniors. and then the seniors are in back."

I nodded. So Kiran and Taylor were juniors and Ariana, a senior. I assumed Noelle was as well. But where had she disappeared to?

"It's so archaic, separating us," Missy said, glancing across at the guys. "What are we gonna do, have sex while they're reading off the morning announcements?"

"Well, *you* might," Lorna joked. She glanced at Missy warily after making her joke, waiting for her reaction.

Missy scoffed, but smiled. Lorna looked relieved.

Sitting on benches up near the lectern were at least two dozen adults, including Ms. Naylor, Ms. Ling, and Dean Marcus, whom I recognized from his picture in the Easton catalog. Clearly the others were teachers, advisors, and deans. Most of them looked stern, judgmental, sour, and wrinkly. A no-nonsense group.

I glanced around for Thomas but didn't see him among the seniors. Hanging on the walls between the windows were long, black velvet banners, each decorated with the Easton crest and a graduating class's year. Below the year were two names, one female, one male. I was about to ask what those names signified when the double doors to the church closed, darkening the room even further. Everyone hushed and faced forward, so I did the same. A sense of heavy reverence descended upon the crowd and an anticipatory warmth overcame me. Out from two opposing doors at the front of the church walked two boys, freshmen from the look of them, carrying candles that they used to light four lanterns near the lectern. These lanterns gave off a surprising amount of light and bathed everyone in a warm, cozy glow.

As soon as the lanterns were lit, there was a hard rap on the door. Dean Marcus stood up and walked slowly down the aisle. He stood, regal and wise, in front of the double doors.

"Who requests entrance to this sacred place?"

I might have laughed if I wasn't in such awe. And if everyone else wasn't so rapt with attention.

"Eager minds in search of knowledge," came the answer. Missy mockingly mouthed the words along with the hidden speaker. Lorna gave her a stern look. Missy rolled her eyes.

"Then you are welcome," the dean said.

"They don't do this every day," Diana whispered to me. "Only at the first service."

The doors swung open and in walked Noelle, chin held high. Next to her was her boyfriend, Dash. His blond hair was slicked

back from his face and he wore a serious expression. He and Noelle
both carried large, antiquated volumes in their arms and kept their
eyes trained directly ahead as they walked down the aisle to the
lectern.

Noelle looked almost regal and certainly in control. Even though
hundreds of people were staring straight at her, she didn't blush or
waver or even blink. She was confident, gorgeous, composed.

The pair placed their books on a table at the front of the chapel.

"Tradition, honor, excellence," they said in unison.

Then they turned to the room and everyone echoed them.
"Tradition, honor, excellence."

Chills rushed over me at the sound of all those voices in unison.
Noelle and Dash turned and bowed together toward the teachers,
then each took a seat on opposite sides of the altar, Noelle in front
of the girls, Dash in front of the guys.

I had no idea what all this ritual meant, exactly, but I loved it. It
was totally different from anything I had ever known before. I was
so enraptured that it took me longer than most to notice the slight
commotion and laughter at the back of the chapel. When I turned
around, Thomas Pearson was just slipping in as the dean closed the
doors. He took a seat in the back pew, where one of his friends gave
him a fist bump and laughed. Sunglasses hid his eyes. The dean
shot him a look of death, but then walked briskly back to the front
of the room. I waited for Thomas to remove the glasses, hoping he
might search me out as well, but instead he grew serious and
trained his attention on the stage.

I turned and did the same, biting down on my lip and trying hard not to laugh. There was something about boys being boys that always made me giddy.

The dean stepped up to the lectern and tilted the microphone toward him. "Welcome, students, to Easton Academy."

SADIST

"Good morning, class! I trust you are all tickled pink to see me."

The teacher banged the door closed behind him and those who weren't already in their seats scrambled. Constance sat down next to me just as the teacher placed his beaten leather briefcase and a tall silver Thermos on his desk. He had the straightest posture I have ever seen and seemed to fill up the entire room. Gray hairs peppered the tight black curls on his head and he wore a blue sport coat and striped tie over tan pants. He clapped his hands together and rubbed them, surveying the room. I could tell by the expressions on my classmates' faces that none of them were actually pleased to see him. From the sarcastic gleam in his eye, it was clear that he was also aware of this fact.

"For those of you who haven't already heard all the nasty rumors about me, my name is Mr. Barber and I am a by-the-book type of man," he said, his voice booming from somewhere in the vicinity of his navel. As he spoke, he twisted off the top of his Thermos and poured himself a cup of steaming liquid. The pungent scent of black coffee filled the room. "This class is American History. In history we have what are known as facts. I teach the facts. We will not be reading opinion or propaganda in this class. We will not be discussing the whining woes of every Tom, Dick, and Harry in every socioeconomic strata of every country around the world. I'll let your college teachers deal with the gray areas. In the meantime, I will prepare you by having you memorize *facts*. Dates. Names. Places. Facts."

I don't think I had ever known anyone who enunciated as perfectly as this man. His jaw must have been working more muscles than my entire body. The word *facts* came out like "fak-t-ss." He took a sip of his coffee and placed the cup down on his desk.

"So let us find out what you know."

Gulp.

He walked to the center of the room, facing us. "You. What's your name?"

"B-Brian Marshall," the towheaded kid in the front row answered. I was surprised he didn't pee on the floor.

"From Mr. Marshall left is team A. The rest of you, team B." Mr. Barber said with a dismissive flick of the wrist. He picked up a pebbled notebook from his huge wooden desk. "I have here the class roster. When I ask you a question, I expect an answer within ten seconds. Answer correctly, your team gets a point. Answer incorrectly, I'll take a point away," he said, eyeing us.

A couple of kids smirked. A couple more looked scared. I had no idea *what* to think. No teacher of mine had ever spoken like this before. This guy had more authority in his little finger than the entire faculty at Croton High combined.

"Let's get started," Mr. Barber said. He looked up and down his class list as he approached the board. Every one of us prayed not to hear our name. "Miss . . ."

Crap. Crap. Crap.

"Talbot."

I glanced at Constance. Her skin grew pale under all those freckles. My heart went out to her even as I was flooded with relief.

"Yes?" she said with remarkable calm.

Okay. If I knew the answer to this, I would be fine.

"Which king of England was served with the lawyer's brief that declared this country's independence in 1776?" he asked.

Wha-huh? Lawyer's brief? Since when was the Declaration of Independence referred to as a lawyer's brief?

Wait. What was the question again?

"King George the third," Constance said.

"Correct."

Constance beamed. Someone behind me said "easy one." Right. King George III had received the Declaration of Independence. I knew that. I just had to focus. I took a deep breath, glad that I hadn't been chosen as the first victim. On the blackboard Mr. Barber wrote a big A and B with bright yellow chalk. Under the B he added a point.

"Next. Mr. Simmons," Mr. Barber said.

"Here," a chunky guy near the door answered.

"Mr. Simmons, who was the first woman executed in the United States and why?"

Okay. That I do not know.

I started to sweat.

"Uh . . . oh. I know this," Simmons said, clutching a pencil in both hands.

You've gotta be kidding me. You do?

"Um . . ."

"Ten seconds, Mr. Simmons." Mr. Barber seemed to be enjoying this. "And for the record, we don't say *um* in my class."

"It's Mary something," the chunky kid said. "Mary . . . Surratt?"

Right. That sounds vaguely familiar. I think.

"Yes. And for what crime was she put to death?"

"Conspiring to assassinate President Lincoln," Mr. Simmons said with much more confidence.

"Good. You pulled that one out, Mr. Simmons," Mr. Barber said, adding a point under the A. I glanced at my watch, wondering if there was any possible way I could make it out of here without getting called on. There were still fifty-three minutes left in the class and only about twenty students.

"Miss . . . Brennan."

Oh, God.

"Yes?"

My mouth was entirely dry.

"I see you're new here," he said with a smirk, looking up from his ledger. Every person in the room turned to look at me. *Thanks. Thanks a lot.*

"Yes," I managed to say.

"I'll give you an easy one, then," Mr. Barber said condescendingly.

I wanted to smack him and thank him at the same time.

Give me something I know. Please just give me something I know.

"How many terms did Franklin Delano Roosevelt serve as president of the United States?" he asked.

Yes!

"Four," I said, grinning.

"I'm sorry. The correct answer is three," Mr. Barber said.

My eyes and face burned with humiliation even as my brain protested. It was four. I knew this. I learned this in eighth grade. FDR was my favorite president. I loved the New Deal and all the acronyms. I memorized them all and aced that quiz. He had served four terms.

"FDR *was* elected for a fourth term, but he died while in office and therefore did not serve four *full* terms," Mr. Barber said.

My entire team groaned as he erased Constance's one point. Under my skin my blood boiled.

"That's a trick question," I blurted.

Mr. Barber froze with his back to us. The students sucked in a breath. My body heat was almost unbearable. What had I just done?

"Excuse me?" Mr. Barber said, turning around.

I cleared my throat. "That was a trick question," I repeated, unwilling to cower. "You didn't ask how many full terms he served."

Mr. Barber was incredulous. He took a few steps forward and crossed his arms over his chest. "I believe the question was fair, Miss Brennan."

I opened my mouth to respond, but he cut me off.

"And why do I believe the question was fair? Because I expect my students to *think*, Miss Brennan," he said. "I expect them to take one moment to consider the options before simply blurting out the first response that pops into their heads. This is not the set of *Jeopardy!*, Miss Brennan; this is your education. You should be more conscientious in the future. Do we understand each other?"

Well. I was officially beaten down. "Ye-yes," I said, my mouth dry.

"I'd like to believe you, Miss Brennan, but perhaps you should see me after class so that we can make sure of that fact," he said.

I swallowed hard. Tears of embarrassment stung my eyes. Every single soul in the room was either staring at me or pointedly struggling *not* to stare at me.

He wanted to see me after class. My first teacher on my first day at the new school that was supposed to change my life wanted to see me after class. Well, something in my life had changed already. I had never been reprimanded by a teacher before. Ever.

"Okay," I said.

"Good," Mr. Barber replied. "Now that we've wasted several minutes of your classmates' precious time, perhaps you would allow me to move on."

I felt hot and sick and stupid. I nodded stiffly. It was pretty much all I could do.

Mr. Barber turned to his next victim and Constance clucked her tongue in sympathy.

Good start, Reed. Really stellar start.

NO EXCEPTIONS

I hovered next to Mr. Barber's desk as he scribbled on a piece of white paper. Everyone avoided eye contact as they filed out of the room, like I was some kind of freak not to be associated with. One class and already I had pegged myself.

"Mr. Barber—"

"I know you are there, Miss Brennan. Kindly allow me to finish."

My jaw snapped shut. I hated him. Even as I wanted to beg him for a second chance. I hadn't been able to answer a single one of the three questions he had posed to me during his sick little game and I knew he thought I was some little-known breed of moron. But what kind of person did that—put students on the wringer on their first day back from summer break? Plus he had humiliated me in front of everyone when he *knew* that I was new here.

Mr. Barber placed his pen down. He took a long, deliberate sip from his coffee cup, then placed that down carefully as well. He was torturing me. He was making me wait here and worry on purpose. Finally, slowly, he tore the top sheet from his pad and held it out to me.

"Some reading for you," he said, looking at me over the top of his glasses. "I expect you to catch up by the end of this week. You should know that I don't take pity on scholarship students. If you do indeed belong here at Easton, you will do the work. No exceptions."

I took the paper, which trembled in my hand. On it was a list of no less than eight books. I wanted to tell him I didn't need to read all this to catch up. I wanted to tell him that I knew the answers to several of his game show questions, but that I had never been good at being put on the spot. I wanted to tell him that his FDR question was a load of shit and that I was fairly certain that he knew it. Most of all, I wanted to tell him that I didn't want to be an exception.

But looking into his watery brown eyes, I knew without question that he wouldn't tolerate me talking back to him again. So all I said was "Thank you."

"And I trust that today's outburst was the last of its kind?" he said.

"Yes, sir," I said.

"Good. You may go."

I turned slowly. I could feel him staring at me as I left the room and wondered what he was thinking. I made myself stand up straight. I couldn't let him think he had broken me.

In the hallway, a couple of girls stood in front of a bulletin board where an orange flyer advertised the Welcome Back Dance, scheduled a few weeks into the semester. I stared at it and wondered if it was even remotely possible that I would be around that long.

No.

None of that.

No negativity. No pessimism. I was going to catch up in this class. I would catch up in everything. Even if I had to work all night, every night, I would do whatever it took to stay at Easton. The alternative—going back to Croton a failure and proving my mother's rantings right—was inconceivable.

Instead, I was going to prove to Mr. Barber that he was wrong about me. His chagrin would just be an added perk.

FIRST ENCOUNTER

When I returned to the cafeteria, a mere five hours after my first trip there, my attitude had completely reversed itself. That morning I had felt hopeful and determined. Now I was exhausted and overwhelmed. As I joined the other girls from my floor at our table—the same one we had claimed that morning—I realized my latest and possibly most alienating mistake of my superterrific morning. On my tray was a heaping bowl of macaroni and cheese and a large Coke, plus three chocolate chip cookies. Their trays? Nothing but salad and diet Cokes. Constance had already hidden her one cookie under a napkin, no doubt in an act of self-preservation.

"Do you know how many fat calories are in that?" Missy said, flicking her gaze at my food.

I dropped into the last empty chair at the end of the table and let my heavy book bag thud to the floor. I decided not to care what Missy Thurber thought of my food. I was too hungry to care. And besides, it was comfort food. If there was one thing I needed just then, it was comfort.

"Pass the ketchup?" I said.

Missy groaned as Kiki handed it over. "Your funeral," Missy said.

Constance pulled her cookie out, bit into it, and smiled at Missy. Missy rolled her eyes and turned her back on us to gossip with her minions.

Constance was starting to grow on me.

"How were the rest of your classes?" she asked sympathetically. Translation: "I already know history sucked. Did it get any better?" Answer: Definitely not.

"Fine," I said with a quick smile.

Even though my French class had been conducted entirely in French and I hadn't been able to keep up or form any coherent answer other than *"Je ne sais pas."* Even though my art history elective had been packed to the rafters with teen curators, all of whom knew the artist, year, and medium of every work our teacher flashed up on the screen. I could only imagine what was going to happen in my next class—Trigonometry. We'd probably skip right to Calculus because everyone would be bored by sines and cosines.

"I know this is going to sound obnoxious or something, but if you ever need any help, I'm totally there," Constance said. "The school I went to back in the city was really good. Like *really* good."

Okay. Was she offering to help me, or showing off? Neither one made me feel any better. It was as if everyone here had decided that I was stupid and in need of charity or something, but I wasn't. I was a straight-A student for God's sake. *I* was the one who always helped out everyone else. What was happening to me?

The girls at my table gabbed about the boys in their classes

and planned a trip into town for the weekend. I overheard the
phrases "four-ply cashmere," "so hot," "new credit card." They
were stressed about nothing. I was stressed about a zillion and one
various things of all shapes and sizes and urgencies.

And then I saw them. The Billings Girls had emerged from the
lunch line and were walking down the aisle right toward us. Noelle
led the way, with Kiran, Taylor, and Ariana trailing behind, her head
bent as she read from her book. For the first time, I could see them
up close and each was more perfect and beautiful than the last.

I held my breath as Noelle sauntered by, her eyes sliding over
me and an amused smile playing around her lips. Kiran and Taylor
chatted their way past and then came Ariana. She wore a white tank
and a long, flowing aqua-colored skirt that grew darker in color
from waist to foot. Around her neck was a sheer purple-and-lavender
scarf, the ends of which hung down over her chest and grazed her
stomach. I would have looked ridiculous in an outfit like that—like
a kid playing dress up—but she *belonged* in those clothes. She
brought with her an exotic scent that still somehow felt familiar.
I was just trying to place it when she lowered the book, looked
directly into my eyes, and said, "Oh. Hello."

All her friends stopped. So did my heart.

"This is the girl I was telling you about," Ariana said. She had the
slightest of southern accents, so muted that it was as if she added it
as an afterthought.

My empty stomach churned and I tasted bile in the back of my
throat. I could feel the girls from my floor looking at one another.

"*Really?*" Noelle crossed her arms over her chest and strode over to me, looking me up and down. A few other girls from Billings, those not of the four, stood back and glanced at one another quizzically. "You're our peeping Tom?"

Missy bleated a laugh.

"I thought she'd be more butch," Kiran said. Taylor laughed, then snorted, then covered her mouth with her hand. Kiran rolled her big, beautiful, perfectly lined eyes and smiled. At me.

"Don't mind her. We're still working out the kinks," Noelle said. "What's your name?"

"Reed," I said.

"I'm Noelle. This is Kiran and Taylor and Ariana," she said. I noticed that she did not bother to introduce any of the other girls from her dorm. So they *were* second string.

"Hi," I said. They smiled. I was on top of the world.

"Now that you know who we are, maybe you can have a little respect and quit licking the glass."

Laughter surrounded me and Noelle smirked at my now blood-less complexion. The Billings Girls smiled superiorly, looking at me with practiced condescension.

"Come on, you guys," Noelle said, turning away. Kiran and Taylor fell in at her sides and they walked off together, like a moving wall. All the others followed—everyone except Ariana, who tilted her head apologetically, looking somewhere over my shoulder.

"Sorry," she said. "Noelle can be a little blunt."

"Yeah," I managed to say.

She tucked her wispy hair behind her ear. Like me, she wore no jewelry or makeup, but still seemed more sophisticated than I ever would be. Her skin was so pale that I felt that if the sun from the skylight shifted, I'd be able to see right through her. For a moment she refocused her blue eyes directly on mine and I saw with perfect clarity that they were sad, even though she was smiling.

"Well, see you," she said finally.

Then she turned her attention to her book again, and trailed off after her friends. Already I wondered if I had imagined the sorrow. Of course I had. What would a girl like her have to be sad about?

"Way to piss off the Billings Girls on your first day," Missy said.

"Were you really spying on them?" Constance asked.

"Not exactly," I replied, privately cursing myself.

What was wrong with me? All I had done since I had arrived here was dig myself a hole. With the teachers, with the Billings Girls. Now I was going to have to do everything I could to scramble out.

LUCK

"Hey, new girl."

As we were on our way out of the cafeteria, Thomas Pearson pushed himself away from the gray brick wall and fell into step with me. Constance shot me a look like *Hello, supah-stah.* Like how could I possibly know a guy this hot on only my second day there?

Search me.

"Hello," I said coolly. Even though my pulse was racing.

"Got something for you," Thomas said.

He produced a small medallion from his pocket. It was bronze and had a square hole in the center. He held it up between his thumb and forefinger, looking quite pleased with himself.

"What is it?" I asked, pausing.

"My good luck charm. I've decided to give it to you because I no longer need luck. I have transcended luck."

I smirked and tried to sound unimpressed. "Good for you." My heart was pounding.

"It is, isn't it?" he replied.

I had to struggle to keep from grinning doofily in his presence. So annoying.

"But really," I said. "What is it?"

"It *was* a subway token. From the days before MetroCards," Thomas said, raising his eyebrows.

What the hell was a MetroCard?

"I was devastated when they outmoded them. Call me old school, but there's just something about slipping something solid into that little slot and hearing that satisfying plink, then reaping the rewards. . . ."

He shook his head wistfully and gazed directly into my eyes. I flushed. Hard. Metaphor intended? Probably. Metaphor noted? Definitely. Girl intrigued, yet mortified? You bet.

"Anyway," he said, breaking the momentary trance. "You hold in your hands a relic from another time. Keep it well."

"Thanks."

He backed away toward the quad, hands in his pockets, grinning suggestively. I caught more than a few girls staring at me with unabashed envy. Hearts broke all across the campus. As Thomas turned away, two guys jogged to catch up with him. He ducked his head and listened as they scurried to keep up.

"*Who* was *that*?" Constance asked with inflection that befitted the magnitude of the man.

I grinned. "That was Thomas Pearson."

"What's his deal?" she asked, standing on her tiptoes to watch him as he and his cohorts were enveloped by the crowd making their way to afternoon classes.

"I have no idea," I said. "Explain to me what this is."

Constance laughed. "You used to use them to pay for the subway. Now they have electronic passes called MetroCards. Geez, Reed. Haven't you ever been to New York?"

No. I'd never been anywhere. Not that she needed to know that.

I stared down at the tiny token, feeling indescribably happy until I felt someone watching me. When I looked up, I was looking directly into Ariana's clear blue eyes. She was a dozen yards away near the stone benches at the center of the quad, but from the intensity of her stare, she may as well have been on top of me. My heart skipped a disturbed beat and I smiled automatically—uncertainly. Then she blinked and turned away, leaving me wondering if I had misread the whole thing.

DEFENSIVE MANEUVERS

I was the first person on the bleachers for soccer practice that after-noon. Not wanting to be late, I had run back to Bradwell after the last class to change, pausing only to slip Thomas's token onto my silver chain and fasten it around my neck before sprinting all the way up the hill to the fields. Now, as the rest of the team approached in one clump, carrying soccer balls and orange cones, I realized that being super-early was just as conspicuous as being late. At the front of the pack, Noelle eyed me as if my appearance amused her.

I pulled my legs closer to me and looked off across the soccer field, avoiding eye contact. Maybe if I *pretended* I was invisible . . .

"Hey, glass-licker," she said, rattling the metal steps as she climbed up. She sat directly behind me, her bare knees straddling my back. I was already sweating beneath the merciless sun, but with her so sitting close to me, I felt new rivulets of sweat start to form. "You play? Or are you just following me?"

A few of the other girls laughed. My face burned. This was going to be way fun.

"All right, ladies! Let's settle down." A middle-aged woman with broad shoulders and calves stood at the bottom of the bleachers. I took this to be the coach. She had short blond hair, wore no makeup or jewelry, and had plenty of dirt under her fingernails. Her eyes fell on me. "You're Reed Brennan, I assume. I'm Coach Lisick."

"Hi," I said.

"Reed comes to us from Pennsylvania where she was the leading defensive scorer in her division as a freshman," Coach announced to the group.

Great. Now Noelle knew I was from good old, square, boring PA. I wondered if I could lie and say I was from Philly. Was there any cachet at all in being from Philly? My guess was no.

"Which means you should all be grateful to have her here," Coach continued. "Got it?"

There was a murmur of assent.

"Glass-licker got skills," Noelle whispered, her breath hot on my ear. "You go, glass-licker."

She patted me twice on the shoulder, hard, and I sunk lower in my seat. There I stayed, feeling her eyes on the back of my neck, until Coach blew the whistle and set us out to scrimmage. I ran out onto the field, relishing the freedom from Noelle's scrutiny. Out here I could do anything.

We lined up on opposite ends of the field, me defending the north goal, Noelle playing forward on the south. We were going to go head-to-head, no question, and my skin sizzled with anticipation. Bring it on.

The whistle blew and Noelle got control of the ball. Naturally. She quickly booted it across to the teammate on her right, who took it upfield. Color me impressed. I had assumed Noelle was a ball-hog type. All glory, no teamwork. Apparently I was wrong.

Noelle streaked toward me and I backed up fast, but she blew by me. The girl was quick. The second Noelle hit open field, her team-mates passed her the ball and my heart lurched. I charged her from behind. I couldn't let her think I was some talent-free plebe. I couldn't let her intimidate me. Not out here.

I raced in and slide-kicked from her blind side, knocking the ball away from her and toward my teammate across the field. Noelle shouted and tripped over my shin guard, hitting the ground hard and tumbling butt-over-head. For a moment our legs were entan-gled, but I extricated myself quickly and stood.

"Nice play, Brennan!" Coach shouted from the sidelines.

I smiled and offered Noelle my hand. But when I looked into her eyes, my heart slammed to a halt. She spat on the ground and glared right through me, seething.

I should have been running downfield after the play, but I couldn't move. Cheers erupted near the far goal and Coach blew the whistle. Noelle shoved herself up from the ground and all I could think about was the fact that she was going to kill me. Kill me dead. For that split second, all the viciousness she was capable of was dis-cernable in her eyes and for some reason I thought of that scar under her clothes, so violent and red. No longer did it seem so very out of place.

But then she faced me and smiled. A genuine, amused, almost proud smile. She brushed the dirt off the front of her shorts.

"Keep doing that and we might win a few this year," she said.

"Thanks," I replied, hoping she'd miscredit my breathlessness to exertion rather than fear.

"But do that to *me* again and we're gonna have a problem."

Then she laughed and ran up to join the rest of the team. I stood there, trying to get ahold of myself, trying to decide if it was too soon to be relieved. Was she irritated with me or impressed?

Somehow I had a feeling that with Noelle, I might never know.

TRUST ME

The other sophomores on the team took off right after practice, so I walked back to Bradwell alone. I wasn't sure why my peers had decided to alienate me. Because I was new? Because Coach had singled me out? Because they felt like it?—but I wasn't surprised. *Alone* was my natural state of being. For now.

I hoisted my gym bag on my shoulder as I came around the building toward the front door. The moment I got there, Ariana stepped out from the alcove, scaring me nearly to death.

"Hey," she said. She clutched a couple of notebooks to her chest.

"Hi."

Was she waiting for me?

"How was practice?" she asked.

"Fine," I said. This was strange. I wasn't sure what I was supposed to do or say. I racked my brain and came up with a fabulously original question. "What team do you play for?"

At Easton, everyone had to play at least one sport. Something about fulfilling a physical fitness requirement. I didn't pay much attention to it because I would be playing, sports requirement or no.

"Oh, I don't," she said. Then, off my confused look, "Health reasons."

"Oh." She didn't elaborate and I didn't feel like she wanted me to ask. Of course, now I had one more thing to obsess about. What could Ariana possibly have that would preclude her from fulfilling her physical fitness requirement?

"So . . . making friends?" she asked.

"I guess," I said.

"How's your floor?" she asked.

"It's . . . good," I said. Constance seemed okay and Diana was nice enough.

"What about guys?"

My mind instantly flashed on Thomas and I felt the cool metal of the subway token against my sweat-caked skin. The Billings Girls had to respect a girl who caught the attention of a hot senior on her first day at Easton, didn't they?

"Well, I met this one guy . . . ," I said.

"Thomas Pearson," she said flatly.

I blinked, surprised. Her tone had all the warmth of black ice.

"I saw you guys talking," she explained. She stepped away from the door, closer to me, as a few girls returned from field hockey practice, laughing and rehashing a play. I felt a flash of jealousy.

"Reed."

"Sorry," I said. What was I thinking, letting my attention

wander from the one person who had been nice to me today? The one person whose attention I would kill for.

"So, you like him?" Ariana asked.

"I haven't decided yet," I said, even though my pulse raced at the very thought of him. Thomas was gorgeous, no doubt. And intriguing and funny. But he was also clearly a player. And I wasn't totally sure I wanted to get involved with someone like that just then. Flirt with? Fine. Get involved with? Another story.

Ariana's eyes narrowed. "Most girls can't resist a guy like Thomas Pearson," she said. "He has that . . ."

Ridiculously sexy quality?

"Dangerous thing going," she finished.

She gazed at me intently, as if gauging my reaction to this assessment.

"Yeah, I could see that," I said nonchalantly. Beautiful and rich and smart and cocky and lascivious? Yeah. That added up to dangerous. "If you go for that type of thing," I added. "Which I don't."

Normally.

But even if I was considering potentially going for it now, she didn't need to know that. Especially if she, for some reason, had some kind of problem with Thomas, as her tone suggested. Besides, the last thing I wanted to do was come off as boy crazy. I wanted to come off as cool. Sophisticated. Above it all. Like she was.

Ariana smiled slowly and seemed to glow from within. "You should sit with us tomorrow," she said. "At breakfast."

My heart didn't beat for a good five seconds.

"Really?" I said, sounding a little too excited.

"I'd like to get to know you better," she said. "We all would."

So they had talked about me. Discussed me. Behind my back. The thought was disconcerting. After such a short time on campus, I already had people talking about me.

But wait . . . did I care? This could be the beginning—the beginning of me getting everything I had hoped for. If they had talked about me, great. Apparently they had seen something they liked. Though what that might be, I had no idea.

"Okay then," I said finally, smothering my giddy glee. "I'm there."

BREAKFAST WITH BILLINGS

Ariana was seated alone at her table when I arrived the next morning, wearing a white sundress and a blue scarf. I wasn't sure if she had gotten there early on my behalf, but I was relieved to see her. Approaching her when she was on her own was a lot easier than the alternative. I kept expecting her to look up from her book as I got closer, but she never did. Finally I was left standing there, hovering, feeling awkward. Maybe it *had* been a joke. Or maybe she had forgotten. Could she really not have noticed the shadow I was casting on her pages?

"Uh . . . Ariana?" I said, prickling with heat.

She raised her head, confused. Oh, God. She *had* forgotten. From the look on her face she didn't even know who I was.

"Sorry," I said automatically.

I was about to retreat when her expression cleared and she smiled. "Hi, Reed," she said. "Sit here."

She pulled out the chair next to hers, in the interior of the table. Relief flooded my body, I walked behind her and placed my tray on the table, then hung my bag on the back of the chair.

"Not hungry?" she said, eyeing my meager breakfast of dry toast and coffee.

Starving, actually. I just hadn't been sure what would constitute a sanctioned breakfast at the Billings table, so I had played it safe. On Ariana's tray was a half-eaten fruit cup, two pieces of toast, and a bowl of dry Lucky Charms. My stomach grumbled at the sight of it all—inaudibly, thank God.

"I'm not a big breakfast person," I lied. Then wanted to kick myself when I realized that if I ended up sitting here again, I was going to have to stick to that.

"I love breakfast," Ariana said lightly, picking up one purple horseshoe marshmallow and placing it in her mouth. "I would eat it three times a day if I could."

I smiled. Her serenity had a calming affect on me. "It's quiet here in the morning," I said, looking around as students trailed blearily in through the double doors.

"That's why I like it," Ariana said. "Much better for reading."

Just then, two girls walked over and took the two opposing seats at the far end of the table. I recognized them from the Billings crowd on my first morning. One had dark skin, jet-black hair, and a Victoria's Secret—worthy body under her jeans and white shirt. The other had straight blond hair that hung halfway down her back. Her outfit was trendy, but a touch *too* trendy, as if she had spent far too much time finding the exact right belt to match the exact right bag to match the exact right shoes. Both shot me confused looks as they sat.

"Hi," the girl said as she removed a magazine from her bag. *The National Review.* There was a picture of the Democrat donkey on the cover with a noose around its neck. No one I knew ever read political magazines. Not even the adults. "You are?"

"This is Reed," Ariana answered before I could. "Reed, that's Natasha Crenshaw and Leanne Shore."

"Hi," I said with a nervous smile.

"Does *Noelle* know you're sitting here?" Leanne asked with a sneer.

My smile drooped.

"She's about to," Ariana said coolly.

Just then, Noelle emerged from the food line, trailed by Taylor, Kiran, and Dash. She smiled hungrily at us and my stomach turned. What had I been thinking, believing that this was a good idea?

"Good morning, glass-licker!" Noelle said, dropping her tray across from Ariana.

My face went red instantly. *Bad idea. Big bad idea.*

"Glass-licker?" Leanne said. "Oh! Right! You're the *les*bian," she said in a husky voice. Natasha smirked as she opened her mag and Leanne laughed, enjoying her own joke.

Ariana brought her book down and glared not at Leanne, but at Noelle. Amazingly, Noelle blushed as well. Ariana could make Noelle blush. Good to know.

"*Sorry!*" Noelle said, rolling her eyes. "Hi, *Reed*," she said pointedly. Then she sat down and scoffed. "Touchy, touchy." She slung her bag over her chair and rolled her eyes. "God, Leanne. Can you shut it?"

Leanne's mouth snapped closed, silencing her laughter. She turned beet red under her makeup.

Ariana brought her book back up and continued to read. It was all I could do to keep the grin off my face. Kiran took a chair across the way and flipped open her Sidekick. Around her neck a large diamond pendant flashed in the sun, nearly blinding me as she settled in. She wore a tiny, soft-looking lemon-colored sweater, black skirt, and kitten heels, all of which screamed *money*. If she sold that outfit, she could probably buy my house with the proceeds. But then I supposed that having your bod on an NYC billboard paid a pretty penny.

Taylor—much more my speed in jeans and a preppy polo—shot me a curious look as she slid behind me and sat down to my right. She did, however, also have large diamond studs in her ears.

"Hi," she said. "I'm Taylor."

"She *knows*," Noelle said impatiently.

Taylor's cheeks turned pink.

"I'm Reed," I said, trying to make her feel better.

"She knows that, too. What are we all, retarded?" Noelle asked.

Natasha sighed and looked up from her magazine. "Noelle. I'd rather you not use that word. At least not around me."

"Sorry, Princess PC. Did you want to slap my wrist?" Noelle said, offering her arm over Kiran's Sidekick. Kiran clucked her tongue and leaned back so she could see.

"That won't be necessary," Natasha said with a smirk.

"Natasha considers herself the moral center of Easton," Noelle told me.

"Well, it's not like any of the rest of you are gunning for the job," Natasha said with false sweetness.

Noelle stuck her finger in her mouth.

Alrighty, then.

"So, Reed, do you like it here so far?" Taylor asked.

"Yeah. Definitely," I said.

"You're from Pennsylvania, right?" she asked brightly. "Is it like your old school?"

I glanced at Noelle. Had she told the others where I was from?

"She already memorized all the textbooks in this place, so she's moved on to yearbooks and new student rosters," Noelle explained.

"Did you know that less that two percent of all Easton students and alumni were from Pennsylvania? Isn't that weird?" Taylor asked. "I mean, considering it's such a big state."

I swallowed hard. Less than 2 percent, huh? So I *was* a huge novelty.

"What do you think of your teachers?" Taylor put in eagerly. "What classes are you taking? Do you have Corcoran for Trig?"

"I—"

"Taylor, you don't need to give her the third degree," Ariana said lightly.

Taylor's face turned pink. "Sorry," she said.

"She needs to know everything," Noelle explained.

"As if she doesn't already," Natasha said under her breath.

Taylor ducked her head, hiding behind her curls, and my heart went out to her. Even though I was relieved to be out from under the microscope.

Just then, Dash dropped down across from me and cleared a curl away from his eyes with a flick of his head. Up close, I could see he was even handsomer than I had realized. With his square jaw, warm brown eyes, and perfect skin he looked like an Abercrombie ad come to life.

"Dash McCafferty," he said by way of greeting. "You're the girl with the sweet feet."

Noelle glanced at me suspiciously.

"You should've seen the way this girl kicked the football the other day," he said to Noelle. "She could give you a run for your money, babe."

"Gee. Sorry I missed it," Noelle said flatly.

Leanne busted out with another laugh until Noelle silenced her with a glance.

A couple of other guys walked over and slapped hands with Dash. One of them sat on the table behind him while the other pulled out another chair and brought it close, as if to be too far away from Dash would have deprived them of oxygen. I recognized both of them from the football game and wondered if Thomas would be far behind.

"This is Josh," Dash said, thumbing over his shoulder at a cute blond kid with a baby face.

"Hey," Josh said with a nod and smile.

"And that loser is Gage."

The taller, trendier kid scoffed. Dash punched him once in the arm—hard, if the contortion of Gage's face was any indication—and that was that.

The double doors opened and I glanced over automatically. Constance and Diana walked in with Missy, Lorna, and the others. Constance scanned the room and I knew she was looking for me, wondering why I had left so early and without her. I felt a stab of guilt as she finally found me and did a double take. I managed an apologetic smile as she walked by me, looking stunned. Missy and Lorna whispered to each other and, if possible, Missy's nostrils flared even wider. The envy was clear.

So far this was a good morning.

"Do you play a lot of sports, Reed?" Taylor asked out of nowhere.

Here we go again. I tore my gaze away from Missy's. Taylor was systematically gutting her bagel, piling all the dough up in a mountain on the side of her tray.

"Just soccer and lacrosse," I said.

"Just like you, babe," Dash said, slinging his arm over Noelle's chair.

Noelle stared at me. "Again I can't help but say, 'Gee.'"

Wow. Guess that respect I gained on the soccer field yesterday really didn't translate to the real world.

Leanne laughed again and Natasha squirmed in her seat. "Leanne, would you kindly remove your nose from my ass? It's starting to chafe," Noelle snapped.

This time, Leanne looked as if she might cry. She got up, pulled her backpack onto her shoulders, and shot me a scathing look before walking off.

"Nice one, Noelle," Natasha said, rising as well. "She just wants you to like her."

I was surprised at the frankness of this statement.

"I'm sorry, Natasha," Noelle said innocently. "But I'm afraid that's going to be impossible."

Natasha rolled her eyes and followed Leanne through the double doors. So all was not harmonious behind the walls of Billings. Somehow, knowing this only made it all the more intriguing.

Someone grabbed the door just before it closed behind Natasha and my heart caught, hoping to spot Thomas. All I saw were a bunch of guys from yesterday's classes. I sat back in my seat and glanced instinctively at Ariana. Sure enough, she had lowered her book and was studying me openly.

"What?" I said, flushing slightly.

"Dash, is Thomas coming to breakfast?" Ariana asked.

My heart practically stopped. What was she, a mind reader? She looked at me meaningfully and I knew for certain that she had asked the question on my behalf.

"Oh God, Ariana. You're not going *there*, are you?" Noelle asked.

"Why? What's wrong with Pearson?" Dash asked.

"I think the more appropriate question is what's *not* wrong with Pearson," Noelle said.

"I was just asking a question," Ariana said coolly. "So, is he coming?"

Dash laughed as he shoveled down a forkful of eggs. "Does he ever?" He glanced at me. "Pearson is *not* a morning person. Ask Josh."

I had no idea why he had directed this comment at me. Had

Thomas said something about me? Or had Dash read my mind and realized who I was looking for as well?

"I'm his roommate. I can attest," Josh said, raising a hand. "Man likes his sleep."

Ariana placed her book aside and picked a piece of toast up from her plate, crunching into it. She smiled at me as she chewed and I smiled back through my embarrassment, silently thanking her for asking the question I never would have had the guts to ask.

"Ugh!" Kiran groaned, snapping her Sidekick closed and tossing it on the table.

She hooked her arm over the back of her chair and looked away from the rest of us for a moment, never once losing her arched posture. Her profile was perfectly angular, her cheekbones sharp and defined. I noticed she also had some kind of shimmer above her eyes, but it was so subtle you could only see it when the light hit her in a certain way.

"Did your technology anger you?" Gage asked.

"Never date a guy from Barcelona," Kiran said, shaking her head slightly as she turned forward again. Every gesture this girl made was elegant and graceful. She picked up an apple wedge, holding it delicately between the tips of her fingers, and took a nibble. "They're gorgeous, yes, but just *so* self-absorbed." Her stunning brown and gold eyes fell on me and she blinked. "Where did *you* come from?"

There was a moment of silence and then everyone else cracked up.

"What? It was just a question," Kiran said.

"She lives in her own little world," Ariana explained.

"Look who's talking," Kiran grumbled at Ariana. She looked me over and leaned back in her chair, placing her apple wedge down on her plate. "You know, this apple is a little sour. I'd like a new one," she said, looking directly into my eyes.

There was a moment of silence and I realized that everyone was looking at me. Expectantly.

"What?"

"She said she'd like a new apple," Noelle said. "And while you're up you can get me a coffee, too."

"And one of those chocolate donuts," Kiran said. "The ones with the sprinkles. I'm celebrating the end of swimsuit season."

"Oooh. I'll have one too," Taylor added.

I looked around at them, my cheeks burning. Were they serious? They were really ordering me to go up and get them food. Dash popped a piece of bagel in his mouth and snickered as he eyed me with amusement.

"Did you get all that or do you need a pad and pen?" Noelle said.

I looked at Ariana. She took a deep breath and continued to read. I was alone here. And I had the distinct feeling that I had no choice.

"All right. I guess I'm going up there, then," I said.

"Good decision," Noelle said.

I rose on shaky legs.

"Aren't you going to ask Ariana if she wants anything?" Kiran said innocently.

Die, die, die.

I paused. "Ariana? Did you want anything?" I asked, making myself sound as pleasant as possible.

"No, thank you, Reed," Ariana said, her tone blithe. Never once did she look up from those pages.

So she was in on it. She didn't actually ask me to sit here so she and her friends could get to know me. They just wanted some new girl they could order around. Well, fine. If that's what it took, that's what I would do.

I turned and walked toward the lunch line, feeling conspicuous and chagrined and humiliated as they all watched me do as they said. But more than anything, I was hoping I wouldn't mess it up. I repeated the order over and over in my mind. Coffee, two donuts, apple.

Wait. Was Kiran's apple red or yellow or green? I paused and glanced over my shoulder to check. Green. Okay. Somehow I knew that if I got it wrong I would never be invited back to their table. And I had to be invited back. I had to be. I'd get them breakfast every morning, I'd endure this lump of humiliation in my chest every day, if they would just invite me back.

DRECK

Later that week, I met with Ms. Naylor right before dinner. She wanted to see how my classes were going—if there was anything I felt was too "challenging" for me. All I could think about was the fact that after my one meal with the Billings Girls, I hadn't been invited to sit with them again. She wanted challenging? Try figuring out how to get back in there. But as important as I knew my social life was, I had a feeling Naylor couldn't care less. As she gazed at me expectantly, I wondered if Mr. Barber had told her about my first day. I imagined them whispering in the faculty lounge or wherever it was adults hung out at a place like this, making wagers on how long I might last. I gave her a tight-lipped smile, told her everything was fine, and resolved to hit the library right away to start in on that list of books he'd given me.

I was not going down without a fight.

It was a humid day with thick gray clouds crowding the sky, the air so heavy it felt as if the atmosphere was pressing in on me from all sides. As always, I walked with my head down and a rivulet of sweat wound its way along my neck and into the collar of my T-shirt. I realized then that I was rushing. Not the kind of weather conducive to rushing. I took a deep breath and slowed down as I made my way around Drake House, a dorm for upperclassmen boys that everyone called "Dreck" because apparently all the unsavory males at Easton lived there.

Everything was going to be fine. I just needed to chill. I just needed to remember why I was here and what I was avoiding going back to. I just needed to—

I rounded the corner of Dreck and heard a window opening, then a giggle. I looked up and stopped dead. There, scrambling out of a basement window and into the bushes, with the help of a large hand on her ass, was Kiran Hayes. She scrambled up, laughing, then straightened her skirt and brushed the dirt from her bare knees. Seconds later, a boy emerged, pulling himself up and tackling her into a kiss. Kiran pushed at his shoulders at first, but then let out a slight moan and kissed him back.

Kiran Hayes was making out with a Dreck boy. The Dreck boy's hands were, in fact, sliding up her tank top toward her breasts.

Right. I didn't need to see that.

I turned to go, but the flash of movement must have caught Kiran's eye. A moment later, she barked.

"Wait! Don't move," she demanded.

I squeezed my eyes shut and turned back toward her, my pulse racing.

"God! You really are a voyeur, aren't you?" she said.

"No!" I wrenched one eye open and caught a glimpse of Kiran's mauler grabbing his book bag and fleeing around the building toward Dreck's front door. It was the tall, gawky kid I had seen her wink at the other day. What was supermodel Kiran doing with a manga-reading loser like that? And I thought she had a boyfriend in Barcelona. "I was just taking a shortcut to the library," I told her. "I didn't see anything."

Kiran's hair was a rat's nest in the back from where it had been pressed up against the rough brick. Her skirt was half turned around and her lipstick was entirely gone, revealing plump, pink lips. I had never seen her look so disheveled, and she was still drop-dead gorgeous.

"Yeah, right," she said, taking a step toward me. "You're not going to tell anyone about this, right?"

"No," I said. "No. Of course not."

"Because you cannot even comprehend the things I can do to you," she said.

Wow. This girl really knew how to cast a threat. Her eyes, so stunningly beautiful on a normal day, were now filled with venom. But even in my intimidated state, I realized that this was a moment I could use to my advantage. I could show Kiran I was trustworthy. I'd been handed another opportunity to prove myself.

"Don't worry," I said. "Your secret's safe with me."

And then, to my surprise, I saw a flicker of relief. She was really scared that people would find out about this. Why? Maybe the kid was kind of a dork, but Kiran was the sort of powerful, popular girl who could get away with dating whomever she wanted and still rise above the snickers and the rumors. Why was she so concerned about keeping this little affair hush-hush?

"Good," Kiran said. "Now go."

No time for questions I'd never have the courage to ask anyway. I turned and got out of there as fast as I could.

FORCE FED

For a while, I had no contact with the Billings Girls, aside from practices with Noelle, at which she mostly ignored my existence. By the third week of school, I was starting to feel hopeless, wondering what I had done wrong. Had Kiran told them to shun me in order to keep me away from them, thereby lessening the chances that I would reveal what I knew? Every time I saw her I wanted to talk to her, to reassure her that I would keep my mouth shut. But every time I saw her, she was with Noelle or Taylor or Ariana and there was no way I could approach them.

Approaching them without an invitation was out of the question.

Meanwhile, it seemed as if the Billings Girls were everywhere. During morning services one particularly hot day, Dean Marcus announced that a very special guest and alumnus of Easton had come to make an announcement, then introduced Lance Hallgren, Oscar-winning superstar and champion, for no apparent reason that I had ever been able to discern, of the U.S. space program. Everyone applauded and murmured as Lance stood before the podium, all big teeth and slick hair, and told us that he was not the only star there that day. That he had graced us with his presence only to present a National Academic Award for Excellence in Scientific Research by a high school student to Taylor Bell. He brought her up to the front of the chapel to thunderous applause, then handed over a plaque and a check for $5,000. The award also came with an all-expenses-paid trip to Washington, where Taylor would present her research during a banquet at the Smithsonian Institution, where she would sit at Lance Hallgren's table.

The biggest academic award I had ever won got me a stiff blue ribbon and a $25 gift certificate to Outback Steakhouse.

That same day, Kiran received a bouquet of two dozen white lilies right in the middle of lunch hour. She passed the card around, so I assumed they weren't from her secret Dreck boy, who sat a few tables away, watching miserably. Moments later, the two delivery men returned, wheeling a lime-green Vespa between them, right into the cafeteria. This got everyone's attention, including the ever-present teachers, who jumped to their feet to interrogate the delivery guys. Instantly everyone was on their feet, theorizing. How did they get that past the gate? Had they paid off security? No one was allowed to have motor vehicles on campus. Would they let her keep it? Like they were going to take anything away from Kiran Hayes. Meanwhile, Kiran had already straddled the Vespa, slipped on the sleek white helmet, and was checking out the features along with Dash, Gage, and Josh, oblivious to all the talk going on around her.

A few days later, one of Ariana's poems was published in the

Easton newspaper—*The Chronicle*—with an accompanying story proudly noting that it had been accepted to be published in *The New Yorker*, which received thousands of submissions from poets of all ages and stages of accomplishment. Then the ballot came out for that year's senior class superlatives, and Noelle's name was all over it. She was nominated for everything from Most Beautiful to Most Likely to Succeed to Class Couple to Best Sense of Humor.

That I had yet to see evidence of.

I glanced over at the Billings table as Diana, Constance, and I emerged from the lunch line on a rainy Tuesday afternoon. Without the sun streaming through the skylight, the cafeteria seemed dim and dank. But still, the Billings girls were the brightest spot in the room.

"Have you picked an artist for your art history project yet?" Diana asked me as we took our seats at the end of our usual table.

"Are you kidding? Our whole room is covered with huge art books she took out of the library," Constance said, taking a sip of her sparkling water. "All she does is stress over them."

Did she think I *wanted* her to tell everyone what I did in the privacy of my own room?

"I just don't want to do someone everyone's done before," I said, lifting one shoulder. "I'm going for originality."

"News flash: Mrs. Treacle is fourteen thousand years old," Diana said. "You are not going to find someone she's never seen done before."

Constance laughed. "I am *so* glad I took journalism," she said.

"Reporting for *The Easton Chronicle* is so much more fun than memorizing a bunch of boring paintings. Plus, my mom knows Mr. Ascher, so I'm definitely going to get a front page story."

Goody for you. Every time I started to like Constance, she said something that reminded me how annoying she could be.

I sighed and glanced over at the Billings table, wondering how I was going to take a whole year of eating three meals a day over here when I had already experienced what it was like to be over there. As if sensing me watching, Noelle looked up and caught my eye. She sighed, shook her head, and pushed herself to her feet. Her chair made a sickening scraping sound.

"What's she doing?" Constance asked.

Noelle was on her way toward our table. My heart was in my throat.

"I don't know."

Noelle stopped right next to us, picked up my tray full of food, turned around, and brought it back to her table without a word. She dropped it next to Kiran and raised her eyebrows at me. Kiran laughed and wiggled her fingers teasingly. Taylor ducked her face behind her curls and flushed. Ariana lowered her book for the first time and looked around, confused. At the far end of the table, Natasha looked peeved and Leanne stared.

"Uh, I think she wants you to go over there," Diana said.

I had to agree. I shot her and Constance baffled looks, then rose and lifted my backpack. Noelle had made quite a scene, so everyone in the cafeteria was now watching my progress. As I slid past Dash and Kiran, I kept waiting for somebody to trip me, for the ground to go out from under me. But nothing happened, and finally I sat.

"If you want to sit over here, just sit over here," Noelle said. "No one's stopping you."

I had a feeling it was the best invitation I was ever going to get. I tried not to look as thrilled as I was.

"Hi, Reed," Taylor said, her cheeks pink.

"Hi," I replied. Ariana smiled at me and returned to her book. Natasha and Leanne ignored my arrival, but I couldn't have cared less.

"So. There's something we need you to do for us," Noelle said.

My heart thumped and I was overcome by a rush of embarrassed heat. Of course. She had only brought me over here to execute some new task. What did she want now? New toast for her turkey sandwich?

"Okay," I said slowly.

"We need you to break up with Kiran's Dreck boy for her."

Kiran went ashen and my heart seized. I looked at her in a panic and saw that her eyes were wide with accusation.

"I didn't tell," I blurted.

Noelle lit up with a grin. "Oh! So you *knew* about it?" she said, looking from me to Kiran. "That's interesting. Are you two, like, confidantes now or something?"

"Noelle," Kiran said. "I—"

"Don't worry. Glass-licker didn't tell on you," Noelle said. "Your little geek has a blog. Were you aware? And he's not too good with the aliases, I must say. One of the guys stumbled across it and e-mailed it to everyone in school last period."

Kiran looked as if she were going to throw up. Throw up, then faint, then die. My heart went out to her.

"A Dreck boy, Kiran. Really," Ariana said, her tone almost sympathetic. "Did you think we weren't going to find out?"

She reached for Kiran's hand in an almost motherly manner. Kiran let Ariana hold her for a moment before pulling away. She swallowed hard and shook her hair back, adopting a nonchalant demeanor. Leaning her elbow on the table, she picked up a carrot stick from her plate.

"Whatever. We were just fooling around," she said. "It's not like I care."

She was lying. We all knew she was lying. But I had a feeling it didn't matter.

"Well, good. Because everyone knows it is unacceptable for a Billings Girl to date a Drake boy," Noelle said. "It's just not done. And since a Billings Girl can't date a Drake boy, it stands to reason that she can't break up with one either. And that, my little glass-licker, is where you come in."

"This should be good," Leanne said.

"Tell him, in no uncertain terms, that it's over," Noelle said, staring me down. "Tell him Kiran no longer wants anything to do with him. Tell him she thinks he's a pasty loser with a puny, shriveled little *thing* and she never wants to speak to him again."

No one moved. I glanced at Kiran. I could tell she was being ripped to shreds inside. And I had the distinct feeling that Noelle had chosen particularly harsh words in order to punish her friend. My heart pounded in my ears, my eyes, my temples.

"That's what you want me to say?"

"Word for word."

I swallowed hard, struggling not to choke. "Now?"

"No. Next Wednesday," Noelle said sarcastically. "Yes, now."

"Uh . . . okay," I said. I looked at Kiran. "What's his name?"

"Like it matters," Noelle said.

"It's James," Kiran replied. She flashed a glance at me and I recognized a glint of desperation. She really did care about this kid. How could she let her friends make me do this? Just because of some stupid image issue? Why didn't she stand up for herself? For him?

I cleared my throat and stood. "I guess I'll . . . be right back."

Slowly I walked over to James's table. Overhead, rain pounded down on the skylight and a flash of lightning briefly lit the room. Everyone in the cafeteria was staring at me. I saw several printed out pages of what must have been James's blog on the tables. When I arrived at the end of the Dreck table, all the guys looked up. Everyone but James, who seemed to be pointedly ignoring me. From the red blotches on his face, he knew I was there, but he kept his attention trained on his manga.

"Uh . . . James?" I said, wiping my hands on my jeans.

"Who are you?" he asked, not looking up.

"I'm Reed," I replied. "No . . . uh . . . Kiran sent me over here."

A couple of the guys snickered and flashed grins at me. James looked up. I saw that he was actually quite handsome, in a pale, lab-troll kind of way. His eyes were a warm brown behind his glasses and he had a kind, if roundish, face.

"Excuse me?" he said, his brow knitting.

I recited what Noelle had said in my mind. There was no way I wanted to tell this poor guy all that in front of his friends, but I knew that I had to. If somehow it got back to Noelle that I deviated from her script, I knew she would hold it against me.

"She said it's over." I pressed my lips together. "She said she no longer wants anything to do with you."

James's jaw clenched. *"What?"*

I took a deep breath and soldiered on. "She said . . . she said you're a pasty loser with a puny, shriveled little thing and she never wants to speak to you again," I said quickly.

"Oh! That's just wrong!" one of the kids at the table cried. A few laughed, but most looked as sickened as I felt inside.

James shoved away from the table, his chair clattering against the empty one behind it.

"Where're you going?" I asked in a panic. At the Billings table, Noelle glared.

"Where do you think I'm going?" he said through his teeth. "If she wants to say all that she can say it to my face."

My heart lurched and I grabbed his arm, stopping him. Somehow I knew that I couldn't let James the Dreck humiliate Kiran in front of the entire school. Somehow I knew that would render this mission a failure. And I couldn't have that. Not now. Not after I had been given a second chance.

"Hey! Buddy! Get a grip!" I said firmly. "I said she doesn't want to talk to you. You were a mistake, all right? A moment of temporary insanity." I glanced over my shoulder at the table, then leaned toward him, lowering my voice to a near breath. "If you go over there, we'll both get ripped to shreds. Don't do it."

I glanced back at Noelle. She eyed me expectantly.

Please, please, please, don't do it, James.

Finally, he took a deep breath and deflated.

"Can you tell her . . . can you tell her I'm sorry?" he asked quietly.

He's sorry? *He's* sorry? Was he kidding me?

"Just don't tell her when her friends are around," he said. "Wait till you're alone."

He understood everything. That much was clear.

"Sure," I whispered, tears stinging my eyes. I was that stunned by my own reprehensible actions. That humiliated by his mature response. I had no idea when I would ever have the chance to get Kiran by herself—I had never seen her without at least one of her friends by her side, except for the time she was with James—but I would do it if I could. I figured I owed this kid that much.

James grabbed his stuff and skulked out of the room, much to the glee of his audience. I was almost surprised when they didn't applaud.

Slowly, I walked toward the Billings table, willing myself not to heave. But when I saw the amused expressions on their faces, the

barely-contained misery on Kiran's, I realized I was in desperate
need of some air. I walked right past them and out the double doors,
pausing under the rain-soaked eaves. Thunder rumbled overhead
and I hugged my stomach, struggling not to cry. What had I just
done?

"Think it'll all be worth it?"

My hand flew up as Thomas pushed away from the wall. His dark
jacket was soaked and raindrops dripped from his hair.

"What the hell? Why are you always lurking?" I demanded,
scared half to death.

Thomas smiled slowly and leaned toward me. Even in all the
roiling emotion, my heart had the temerity to respond.

"Don't get in over your head, new girl," he said. Then he looked
me up and down. The covetousness in his eyes both flattered and
unnerved me. It was as if he believed that I in some way belonged to
him. "I don't think I could handle it."

For a split second he loomed even closer, I could feel his breath
on my face and I knew for sure he was going to kiss me. But instead
he smiled and turned and walked off into the rain.

ALL LIES

Turned out I didn't have to figure out a way to get Kiran alone. When I walked out of Bradwell the following morning with Constance and the others, she stood up from the nearest stone bench in the quad. I could see the nervousness in her eyes.

"I'll see you in class," I told Constance as I split away.

Kiran drew herself up with a breath as I approached. By the time I got to her, any uncertainty was gone and her imperious, blasé demeanor was back in place.

"Hi," I said. My turn to be uncertain.

"What did he say to you?" she asked point-blank. "Not that I care. I just need to make sure that he got the message."

Lies. All of it. Lies.

"He got the message," I told her. "Don't worry."

She stared. The gold flecks in her eyes seemed to pulsate. "Well? What did he *say*?"

I cleared my throat. "He said he's sorry," I told her. "He said to get you alone and tell you that he's sorry."

Kiran blinked. "He said that?"

"Yeah," I told her, my curiosity overwhelming. "Why would he say that after what I did to him?"

"I don't know," Kiran said, shaking her head as she stared past me. She cracked the briefest of smiles. "That's James."

I smiled too. We were sharing a moment here. An actual moment. Kiran was letting me see a part of her that she would never let Noelle and the others see. I was sure of it. Her big eyes suddenly filled with tears.

"Hey. Are you all right?" I asked.

Instantly she refocused. When she looked at me again she was all business. "We never spoke," she said.

My heart thumped. "Where do they think you are?"

"None of your business," she said. She rolled her eyes at my flinch. "Look, I know you didn't tell them about him and I appreciate that, all right?" she said under her breath as if, at that very moment, they were listening. "But I need you to do it again. This conversation never happened. It goes with you to the grave."

What are you so afraid of? What are you so afraid of?

I wanted to scream it, but I bit my tongue.

"Okay," I said.

"Good." She nodded resolutely and slipped her dark sunglasses over her eyes. Just before she strolled off, I could have sworn she muttered a thank-you.

THE HERD

"You're getting enough to eat?" my father asked me.

"Yeah," I told him. "The food here is good."

Not a total lie. It was at least better than the food at Croton High.
I propped my feet up on the small shelf under the pay phone. My
butt already hurt after just two minutes on the small wooden bench.
There were no phone jacks in the rooms, so everyone on the floor
was supposed to use this one public phone. Everyone I knew had a
cell, though. I was the only resident who ever used it.

"I miss you, kiddo," my father said.

It was weird talking to him on the phone. Aside from quick calls to
ask for a ride, I had never talked to him on the phone in my life. I
imagined him sitting at the table in the kitchen, the sports section
open in front of him, and the image depressed me. With my finger I
traced the words "Slayer Rules!" had been etched into the wall.

"I miss you, too, Dad."

"I'm looking forward to parents' weekend," he said. "We
both are."

My heart thumped. I had read about parents' weekend in the Easton Handbook, but I had blocked out its existence. I couldn't imagine my parents here any more than I could imagine them on Mars. I also couldn't imagine them making the drive without my mother bitching and whining the entire time. Why my father actually thought it was an attractive idea was beyond me.

"I'd better go," he said. "Mom wants to eat dinner."

"Okay," I said. Now I saw her sitting there as well, glowering at him over a tray of gray meatloaf.

"She says hello," my father said.

No, she doesn't.

"Okay. Bye, dad," I said.

"Love you, Reed."

"You, too."

I hung up the phone and took a moment to catch my breath. It was amazing how each phone call pulled me back there so entirely. To that misery, that fear, that darkness. Each time I spoke to my father, I had to recompose myself. Remind myself that I wasn't there anymore. And then, just as I did every morning that I didn't wake up to my mother shouting at me from her room to get up and bring her her morning pills, I would smile. My life was my own now. I was still getting used to it.

A rap on the glass door of the booth made me jump. Constance's eager face looked down at me through the foggy glass.

"Come on! You're missing it!" She waved maniacally for me to follow her, then ran. I sighed and hoisted myself up.

It was Sunday evening and all the girls on my floor had gathered in the common room to watch some random reality show. It was all they had talked about all day. I had never seen it before and that was the subject of at least half an hour of incredulous conversation after dinner. Now I was finally going to see what all the fuss was about.

Couldn't wait. Really.

I plopped down on the loveseat next to Constance, who had saved me the space. As soon as the first commercial appeared, Lorna turned from her spot on the floor. She was seated on a pink silk pillow she had brought down from her room.

"So what do you *do* on Sunday nights?" she asked me. She had some kind of smelly blue mask smeared all over her face, and her curly hair was up in two buns at the top of her head. She looked like some kind of comic book villain. The Blue Terror.

"Read, mostly," I said.

Missy scoffed and Lorna rolled her eyes. These were their two favorite affectations. At any given moment you could find one of them doing one or the other.

During subsequent commercials, Constance updated me on the backstory, but I only half-listened. I knew I should be back in my room or at the library, reading through the extra history texts I had yet to wade through. Or practicing French pronunciation. Or doing trig problems. Pretty much the only class I wasn't feeling stressed about was my lit class, and that was only *because* I spent all my Sundays up until now reading. But as much work as I had to do, I wanted to be social. I needed to be.

Of course, I wished I was spending this time socializing with the Billings Girls, but that was not an option. I had spent my meals with them ever since Noelle had stolen my tray, running for their food and executing every other small errand that popped into their minds, but our contact had yet to extend outside the cafeteria.

"So, everyone going to the dance on Saturday?" Diana asked as the scene faded to black, then to a car commercial. Kiki sat next to her, head bobbing to her personal soundtrack as she flipped through the latest issue of *In Touch*.

"Of course," Missy said. She pushed herself up from the floor where she had been painting her toenails and sat on the couch, capping her nail polish bottle. "I need to pick out my boyfriend."

Like she was shopping for socks.

"We never had dances at my old school," Constance said. "Well, unless you count charity events, but then all the parents were there. There's no parents at this one, right?"

Missy answered with another eye roll.

"We'll take that as a *no*," I said.

"Then I'm definitely there," Constance said. "What about you, Reed?"

I flushed at the very idea of attending a school dance. I had never shown my face at one in Croton. Only the cheerleaders and male jocks went to them and later they were always crashed by the burnout crowd and eventually closed down early by the cops. As a result, they had dwindled from four a year to exactly one—the prom—which was only for juniors and seniors. As a result, I had never danced with a boy in my life. Not once.

"I don't know," I said. "I actually have a lot of work to do."

"You read on Sundays *and* you're gonna do homework on a Saturday night?" Lorna said, cracking her mask as she pulled a face. "Back up, ladies—we have a party animal."

"Don't bother with the reverse psychology, Lorna. There's no way she'll go," Missy said, going to work on her cuticles with a pair of cuticle scissors.

"What's that supposed to mean?" I asked.

"It means, you're a sheep," she said, looking me in the eye. It was all I could do to keep from staring down the deep caverns of her nostrils. If I looked long enough, would I be able to spot the blackness of her heart? "There's no way the *Billings* Girls are going to go, because they think they're all above any and all school functions, and we all know that whatever they do, you'll do. Isn't that what sheep do? Follow the herd?"

Lorna snickered along with her friends. Constance bit her lip and glanced warily in my direction, wondering if I was going to explode.

There were about a million things I could have said. I could have pointed out the fact that she was just jealous that the Billings Girls knew I existed. I could have reminded her that she was the one who was so looking forward to being a Billings Girl next year, and if she so wanted to be one, why was *she* going to the dance? But I knew that whatever I said would come off as a defensive rant.

I wasn't going to give Missy Thurber the satisfaction. Even though my blood was boiling hot enough to spew lava, I just stood up without saying anything and calmly walked back to my room, wondering why I had ever craved the friendship of other girls.

LIAR

"Are you going to talk to him?" Constance asked me breathlessly.

I stood against the wall of the great room, where Easton apparently held all their events from fundraisers to blood drives, staring across the room at Thomas, who was surrounded by people. Freshmen and sophomores mostly, since it seemed that most juniors and seniors had avoided this, the first school dance, including—as predicted—the Billings Girls. Missy was right. They were above events like this. Far too sophisticated, too cool, too blessed with thousands of better things to do. I had come for exactly three reasons: 1) because Constance had begged me to, and I knew she would never let it die until I said yes; 2) because Missy had publicly declared there was no way I would show; and 3) because I myself had nothing to hold me back other than a stack of homework the size of a Buick.

What I didn't get was why Thomas was there. If the Billings Girls were too good to be here, he certainly was as well.

"I might," I said.

If he wasn't so clearly otherwise occupied.

I watched with a pang of jealousy as a pretty, petite brunette laughed at something he said. Ever since that look Thomas had given me outside the cafeteria, I hadn't been able to stop thinking about him. Even though I knew he was probably trouble, I just felt a deep pull toward him and a sense of connection that was weirdly powerful considering how few times we'd actually spoken. But the heart wanted what it wanted. And tonight it definitely wanted Thomas.

All around the room, people kept to the walls, talking and laughing or staring out at the empty dance floor while the DJ spun random dance hits of the last ten years. A few teachers roamed the periphery, staring people down and looking generally peeved. It seemed as if Easton had tapped its sternest adults to chaperone the event, and I wondered if anyone would be dancing or at least having some kind of fun if these sentries of doom weren't present. All in all, it probably would have been the lamest dance I had ever been to. If I had ever been to a dance before.

"Why don't you just go ask him to dance?" Constance said.

"Uh, no one else is dancing," I said.

"Well, then, at least go say hello," Constance said. "C'mon. We need some romance around here and it can't be me since I have, you know, Clint. I need to live vicariously through you."

"Look, I never even said I liked the guy," I said.

She scoffed. "Yeah, right. It's, like, so obvious."

Oh, God. Was it? How humiliating.

"I don't see what the big deal is," Missy said, horning in on the

He's just a person."

Right. Like you could do it.

"A person who's coming over here," Constance said under her breath.

What? I looked up. Slowly, Thomas was making his way across the room. He looked right into my eyes and smiled the whole way.

He stopped right in front of me and tucked his chin. "Where's your entourage?" he asked.

"My entourage?"

"The Billings Girls," he said. "I thought you didn't leave home without them."

Behind me, Missy snorted. Was this why he had come over here? To mock me?

"I do what I want to do," I said, lifting my chin slightly.

"Good," he replied. "You don't need them anyway."

Yes, I did. And if he didn't realize that, he was a lot more clueless about this school of his than he knew.

"Well, someone should be dancing," he said. "And I think that someone is Reed Brennan." He smiled slowly and offered both his hands.

Damn.

"But . . . no one else is dancing," I said.

"What's the matter? You scared?" he asked.

I narrowed my eyes. "Please."

I took his hands and he backed toward the dance floor, watching my eyes the whole way. Everyone in the room stared. The teachers looked almost disgusted that someone actually had the gall to dance at this dance. The guys seemed merely intrigued, but

I could practically *taste* the jealousy radiating off the female population. The hottest guy there, the only guy with the guts to actually dance, had chosen to dance with me.

Thomas paused. My heart pounded in my every pore. Without a word, he lifted my arms and placed them around his neck. Then he slid his arms around my waist, his hands resting lightly just at the small of my back. His eyes never left mine. As we started to step from side to side, my breath grew short. Every inch of me ached to touch him. Arms and hands were not enough.

"What are you thinking?" he asked me, his voice sending reverbs through my chest.

I flushed. "Nothing."

Thomas lifted one corner of his mouth, bringing out a small dimple. "Yes, you were. You were thinking something naughty." My skin sizzled. He brought his cheek to mine and his stubble scratched my skin. His breath was hot on my ear. "Tell me your naughty thoughts, Reed Brennan."

Oh, God. My palms were sweating. My head swam. My whole body throbbed.

"Do I make you nervous?" he asked.

I shook my head.

He pulled back slightly, looked me in the eye, and smiled. "Liar."

And then he kissed me.

DANGEROUS?

I had been hoping that Thomas would actually show up on time for morning services, wanting to see me as much as I wanted to see him, but he sneaked in ten minutes late as usual and hunkered down in his seat with his sunglasses on. Result? I couldn't even catch his eye. How he got away with that stuff, I had no idea, but no one seemed to bother him about it. He was just that type of guy.

I spent the morning "studying" out on the quad in the sun with Constance. I had to do something about my not-so-stellar academic record. When I presented my art history project earlier Friday morning—I had decided to do it on Frida Kahlo—Mrs. Treacle had critiqued it right away as she had all the others, calling it pedestrian and under-researched (unlike all the others). She gave me a C and told me to do better next time. An oral report in French didn't go much better. Although my pronunciation had improved, Miss Krantz said I was still too hesitant and that my lack of confidence was distracting. And finally, there was the history quiz. I didn't even want to think about the number of blanks I had left on that page.

I wanted to buckle down. I really did. But most of my time on the quad was actually spent scanning my surroundings, hoping for a glimpse of Thomas. All I could think about was that kiss. The way he had touched my face with his fingertips. I had never had a kiss like that before. And I wanted more. Now.

"You're thinking about him, aren't you?" Constance asked me during one of my many dazed-in-space jags.

"No. I was just . . . trying to figure out this equation," I said, looking down at my trig book and blushing.

"Yeah, right. You're so in love you can't even stop smiling," she said.

"I'm not in love," I said flatly.

"Yes, you are!" she teased.

"Let's just study," I said.

Constance's face fell and she went back to her work without a word. I instantly felt guilty for shutting her down, but didn't know what to say. When was I going to learn?

I took a deep breath and tried to concentrate. I really did. But five seconds later, I was with Thomas again. I definitely had it bad.

Lunch hour could not come fast enough. Thomas always showed up for lunch, however briefly. I was salivating at the thought of seeing him.

I approached the Billings table uncertainly as I always did, waiting for them to tell me it was all a joke and to go away. When I slipped into my chair without incident, I let out a sigh of relief. Ariana looked up briefly from her book and gave me a wan smile.

"Hi, Reed!" Taylor said brightly, as she always did. She was the only one of the four who always seemed genuinely pleased to see me.

"Hi," I replied.

I glanced at Kiran. She ignored my presence as if nothing out of the ordinary had ever occurred between us.

"How's everything going? How are your classes?" Taylor asked. "Did you do anything interesting yesterday?"

"Fine, fine, and no. Not really," I said lightly. I was getting used to Taylor's questions and learning how to answer them as vaguely as possible.

"Yeah, right. I hear you and Thomas Pearson got nasty last night," Noelle said, amused.

My mouth opened slightly, but nothing came out. How did she always know everything?

"Thomas Pearson?" Kiran said, raising one perfect eyebrow. "*There's* a good idea."

Right. Like your Dreck boy was such a wise choice.

"Did you know that the Pearsons donate two hundred and fifty thousand dollars to the school every year? That's on top of his tuition," Taylor offered.

Two hundred and fifty thousand dollars? Two hundred and fifty *thousand dollars*?! How rich *were* these people?

"Taylor. Really," Ariana scolded. As if talking about money was just that wrong.

And as always, Taylor clammed up.

Just then the double doors opened and Thomas walked in with

Dash, Gage, and Josh. My heart caught and immediately began racing. I was expecting to *maybe* catch him in the last ten minutes of the meal when he usually appeared, grabbed food, and bailed. But there he was, trailed by his friends. Right on time.

I told myself not to expect anything. Maybe the kiss meant nothing. Maybe he had forgotten I existed. Maybe he—

"Hey, new girl," he said, sliding into the chair next to mine. He pushed my hair back from my face with his fingertips and when I turned to him, kissed me right on the lips. "I guess I should start calling you Reed now."

Now. As in, 'Now, because everything as changed.' 'Now, because you are my girlfriend.' *Whoa*.

"Yo, Josh. You going up there?" he asked, resting his arm on the back of my chair. Shivers all over.

Josh hesitated in the aisle as Gage and Dash walked ahead. "Yeah."

"Get me a sandwich, all right? I'm starving," Thomas said. Then he brought his face to mine and kissed me again. I could *feel* Kiran and Taylor whispering across the table.

"Do I look like your butler?" Josh asked.

Thomas broke off and glared at him. "Yeah, actually, you do."

Josh colored slightly, then rolled his eyes and walked off.

"So, Pearson. Found yourself a new victim?" Noelle asked.

My breath caught. What did *that* mean?

"Ironic statement, coming from you," Thomas said.

Noelle reddened. "I'm surprised you know what *ironic* means."

"Shut it, Lange," Thomas snapped.

"Hey. Watch it, dude," Dash said, returning to the table.

Thomas glared at him for a second, then laughed snarkily and kissed my cheek. What was that all about?

"What is up with the selection today?" Dash asked. "There's no hot food."

"Maybe because it's ninety-five degrees outside?" Kiran suggested, checking her reflection in her ever-present compact.

"Think fast," Josh called out.

I ducked out of the way as a cellophane-wrapped baguette sandwich zoomed past my face. Thomas grabbed it effortlessly.

"Premade? We're so lucky to be the over privileged souls we are," he joked.

My stomach shifted slightly. I wondered if he knew that I didn't fall into that category. If any of them knew. If they'd care.

"I cannot *wait* for parents' weekend," Gage said, tearing into his own sandwich.

Thomas blew out a sigh and dropped back in his chair. Instant attitude shift.

"Why? What's so great about parents' weekend?" I asked. I was curious as to what went on, wondering if it was even remotely possible that my parents would fit in. And if I could possibly avoid them the entire time they were present.

"Gage is referring to the fact that it's the best food of the year," Noelle explained. "His world revolves around his stomach."

"And areas slightly further south," Gage added, laughing with his mouth open so that we could all see his half-chewed food.

"I just can't wait to see my mom," Ariana said.

"Ladies and gentlemen, here she is. The only girl who thinks the

worst part of boarding school is being away from her parents,"
Noelle announced.

Everyone laughed except Thomas. "Can we talk about something
a little less boring please?" he asked.

"Touchy, touchy," Kiran said as she continued studying herself
from every angle.

"You just sound like a bunch of losers," Thomas grumbled. "It's
a stupid tradition. I don't know why they even bother anymore. If
our parents want to send us shit, they can use the Internet. Why
disrupt everything for an entire weekend?"

"Dude, chill. It's not our fault your parents are assholes,"
Dash said.

"Screw you, jackass," Thomas snapped.

And the last of the mirth was obliterated. I flushed, shocked.
Clearly Thomas had parental issues. He had grown blotchy around
the neckline of his shirt and looked skittish, as if ready to bolt at the
first loud noise.

"Are you all right?" I asked him.

"I'm fine," he said, taking my hand. He looked at me with
pleading eyes. "Let's get out of here."

I didn't want to go, really. Meal times with the Billings Girls
were the best parts of my day. But he looked desperate, and his foot
was bouncing up and down under the table, and he wanted me to
leave with him. Me.

"Sure," I said.

He got up quickly and pulled me out of there so fast I barely had
a chance to blurt a good-bye.

FAMILIAR

Thomas shoved through the cafeteria doors, stormed over to the closest tree, and slammed his fist into the bark.

"Thomas!" I shouted.

He didn't even seem to hear me. He pulled back and smashed his fist into the tree trunk again. And again and again.

"Stop it!" I shouted, grabbing his arm.

He resisted me at first, but then stopped when he saw how scared I looked.

"What's going on?" I asked.

Pointless question. But my heart was pounding and I felt almost weak with fear and concern. I had to say *something*.

Thomas blew out a breath and dropped down on a stone bench facing the cafeteria. He threw his bag down on the ground. Overhead, clouds raced across the sky and a cool breeze sent chills down my back.

"Sorry. Sorry," Thomas said, stuffing his damaged hand under his arm.

"It's okay," I told him. It wasn't as if I'd never witnessed a melt-down before. "Just take a deep breath."

He shot me a grateful glance and did as I said, looking away from me. Clearly he was holding back. Whatever the freak-out was about, he hadn't gotten it out of his system.

"Dammit," Thomas said under his breath.

I put my hand on his back, but he flinched away. My face felt hot. Did he want me to go? *Should* I go? I didn't want to leave him alone. Just in case. In the midst of my self-contradiction, I heard someone whistling.

Perfect. One of the teachers strolled down the path toward us. I cursed under my breath.

"Don't say anything," Thomas pleaded, sounding very much like a little boy afraid of getting in trouble. My heart went out to him.

"Don't worry."

The elderly teacher paused and looked down at us. He wore a bowtie and a tweed wool jacket with a recently plucked wildflower sticking out of the buttonhole in the lapel. His white mustache twitched when he spoke. "Everything all right here, Mr. Pearson?"

"Fine. Fine, Mr. Cross," Thomas replied.

"Shouldn't you be in lunch now, Mr. Pearson?" he asked.

"My friend here was feeling a little nauseous so I brought her outside to get some air," Thomas said. So composed you never would have known he'd thrown a hissy two seconds earlier. "This is Reed Brennan, Mr. Cross. She's a sophomore."

"A pleasure to meet you, Miss Brennan," the man said, tipping his head toward me. "Don't stay out here too long."

"We won't," I replied.

When he finally strolled off again, both Thomas and I were able to breathe.

"God, I detest them sometimes," Thomas said.

"Who? Teachers?" I asked.

"No. *Them*," he said, throwing his battered hand up toward the cafeteria. "Freakin' Noelle and Dash. Who the hell does he think he is?"

"I don't know. I . . ." What was I supposed to say here? I'd never seen anyone other than my own mother snap like Thomas just had. And there was never anything I could say to help her. "Are you okay?" I asked, glancing at his hand. His knuckles were bright red.

"Yeah. It's fine," he said. His breath seemed to be slowing and he leaned his elbow on the arm of the bench. "I'm sorry," he said, chagrined. "I just get so pissed sometimes."

I smiled slightly. "I know the feeling."

"You do?" He seemed hopeful.

"Yeah. I normally take it out on a *pillow*, but . . ."

Thomas looked at me. "What do you have to be angry about?" His expression had softened.

I tensed up all over. I had never told a soul about my mother. Not one person. Not one word. But the way he was looking at me, so sweet and concerned, almost made me want to.

"You tell me yours and I'll tell you mine," I said, stalling.

Thomas smiled slightly. Sadly. "Okay. If you really want to know." He looked across at the cafeteria wall. "Where to begin . . . ? Dad's a tremendous drunk and Mom is an insanely tremendous drunk. He gets loud and obnoxious, she gets quiet and snippy, and together they fuck up everything," he said, warming quickly to his subject, like he was relishing getting it off his chest. "We're talking birthdays, vacations, Christmases. At my eighth grade graduation, my father ended up falling asleep with the video camera in his hands and fell out of his chair into the aisle, then yelled at the headmaster for the faulty seats. That made for a stellar little piece of film nostalgia. And don't even get me started on my mother."

I felt my heart tighten in my chest. I recognized his tone. Fed up. Sad. Disappointed. Embarrassed.

"They come up here every year and the whole school kisses their asses because of their money. They get to act all high and mighty for two days and order me around and act the perfect parents and it just makes me sick," Thomas said, blinking back tears. He looked up again and took a deep breath, blowing it out. "This place is mine, you know. And they come here and they just . . . they ruin it for me." He sighed and stared past me.

I sat there for a moment, feeling for him. Feeling for me.

"Your turn," he said.

Oh, God. I looked him in the eye. Hoped I could trust him. Here we go.

"For me it's just my mom," I said, then couldn't believe I had actually said it. "Except she likes pills with her bourbon. Prescription ones. All kinds. So, depending on what color she's popped that day, she's either psychotic or passed out and dead to the world. Plus she hates me."

"I'm sure that's not true," Thomas said automatically.

"No. It is," I said, trying to make it sound like it was no big deal. "She hates me for being here, for having a life, for being young, for being healthy. She was in a car accident when I was eight and her back is all screwed up from it. Still. That's when it all started. Anyway, one time, when she was on a particularly nasty bender, she actually told me all this. How she despises me."

Thomas looked at me, deep into my eyes, and nodded. And that one tiny nod said everything. His eyes looked sad, but not because he was pitying me.

He understood.

After all this time of keeping it in, I'd finally told someone. My heart flooded with relief.

"What about your dad?"

"Oh, I love my dad. Dad's the best," I said. "But my mom, forget about it. If she comes here for parents' weekend, she'll humiliate me just for fun. It'll be miserable."

"So don't ask them to come," he said simply.

I laughed. "*You* don't ask your parents to come."

"Touché." Thomas smiled slightly. Then he reached out and took my hand with his good one. "We're pretty screwed up, huh?"

"We make a good pair," I said.

"Have I told you I'm glad you came here?"

"No," I replied, feeling a smile form on my face.

"I am. In fact, I think we should eat lunch together alone from now on," he said. "Just you and me."

My stomach twisted slightly. "But what about—"

"The Billings Girls?" he said. "Could someone please tell me what's so great about the freakin' Billings Girls?"

I raised my eyebrows.

"I'm just trying to make friends here," I said quietly.

"So be friends with me," he said, moving closer. He kissed me quickly on the lips and my whole body tingled. "Why do you need them when you've got me?"

Because they have everything I have ever wanted. Because they can teach me to be like them. Because if I'm with them I will have a future.

"A girl needs girlfriends," I said simply.

He pulled back. "And you think *they* are your friends," he said incredulously.

I squirmed. "They've always been nice to me."

He scoffed. "Yeah, right."

"They have!" I lied. "The girls on my floor are much worse, trust me."

"I can't believe you'd choose them over me," he joked, shaking his head. "You disappoint me, Reed Brennan."

"Come on!" I said, shoving him with my leg. "I think I can handle all of you."

"If you say so," he said with a blithe shrug. Then he looked me in the eye and grew serious. "I just don't want to see you get hurt."

I was touched, and I smiled. What exactly did he think was going to happen to me? "Thanks. But I'll be fine."

Thomas smiled in return. "I should go get this cleaned up," he said, raising his hand.

"Want me to go to the infirmary with you?" I asked.

"Can't go there. The nurse will have to inform the parents about something like this, and that's the last thing I need," he said, standing. "You go inside. Go back to your precious 'friends,'" he said, air-quoting with one hand.

I laughed and shook my head. But inside I was starting to feel uneasy. Could I date Thomas when the Billings Girls clearly disapproved of him? Could I hang out with the Billings Girls when Thomas clearly thought they were no good? Why did the two most important parts of my life here at Easton have to be at odds?

I looked up at Thomas. All I wanted to do was hug him and protect him and, of course, kiss him. A lot. Whenever humanly possible. There was no way I could give him up. Not now. Not when I finally found someone who understood.

But I also knew that I couldn't endure another scene like today. Another tense lunch. Another smackdown with a tree trunk. I would just have to try to keep them separated. A girl had to make certain sacrifices if she wanted to have it all.

"I'll see you later?" I said.

"Most definitely," he replied. Then he leaned down, kissed my forehead, and was gone.

C IS THE NEW F

On Monday morning at the end of class, Mr. Barber handed back our quizzes from the previous Friday. He walked up and down the aisles, slapping the papers face down on each desk.

"As you may or may not know, I work on what some people call an unorthodox grading system," he said as people grabbed up their quizzes and either groaned or grinned. "In my class there is no C. There is no D. There is only A for excellent, B for satisfactory, and F. You all know what F means. This means that, while quite a few of you have passed this quiz, several of you have failed," he added. He paused by my desk and the pungent scent of stale coffee enveloped me. With a flourish, he handed me my paper, face up toward the room, for everyone around me to see. Red marks everywhere, topped by a big, fat F.

I took the paper from him, hot tears stinging my eyes. He looked disgusted as he turned away. "Those of you who have failed might want to consider spending a bit more time in the library this week. Friday's quiz will feature double the questions."

Mr. Barber sat down at his desk and jotted a few things in his notebook. "Good day," he said, reaching for his coffee. And on cue the bell rang.

I stood up, staring down at the page, doing the math quickly in my head. Thirty-seven of fifty questions right. That was a 74. I had gotten a 74 and received an F. What kind of psycho school was this? How could the dean let Barber get away with this?

Missy scoffed as she walked by me. "Guess we're not in PS 31 anymore, huh?"

One day I was going to shove something up her nostril. Seriously.

"Oooh, sorry," Constance said, wincing as she fell into step with me on the way out the door. "Want to study with me next time? I have this whole flash card system that really works."

I stared at Mr. Barber as she ushered me out of the room, wondering how sad and miserable a person you would have to be to torture innocent kids like this. He must have felt me watching him. Had to feel the heat of my glare. But he never looked up from his book. His refusal to acknowledge me just made me hate him more.

But by the end of the day, I started to wonder if Mr. Barber had been right to give me that F. Several of my teachers handed back grades from last week's work and with each one my heart had sunk lower. Clearly, here at Easton, I was no longer an A student. But at least the other teachers were kind enough to stick to the traditional grading system.

Aside from the C on my art history oral, there was a C+ in

French, a B- in Trig, and a C on an English paper I had written on Upton Sinclair. Apparently even a paper about one of my favorite authors, written for one of my favorite classes, wasn't going to save me. My only A was on a biology lab that had been done in class with three partners, and I can't say I contributed all that much, having stayed up late the night before, whispering with Thomas on the hall phone. I was not at all surprised when, upon receiving my mail that afternoon, there was a note from Ms. Naylor to come see her.

I had a feeling it was time to start packing my bags.

CHANCE ENCOUNTER

On my way to see Ms. Naylor before dinner, I scurried by Gwendolyn Hall, the old class building that had been closed up ten years ago due to problems with its "structural integrity." I was surprised when a trio of guys stepped out from behind the back wall and hurried off toward the quad, but I kept walking. Until I heard his voice.

"Hey."

My heart caught. It was Thomas. He leaned back against the stone wall with one knee crooked, his foot pressed into the rock behind him. He held out his hand to me.

"C'mere."

A rush of warmth overcame me. I glanced over my shoulder at Hale Hall, which the students called "Hell Hall" since that was where the advisors and teachers kept their offices. If I hesitated for very long, I would be late. But not even my fear of Naylor could tear me from the mischievous longing in Thomas's eyes.

I took his hand.

"Where're we going?" I asked.

He said nothing. He pulled me around the corner and up a set of crumbling stairs, through an open stone doorway. On the other side was an outdoor room that was almost like a cave, the walls wet with dew. Somewhere nearby drops dripped a constant beat. Thomas sat down on a bench built into one of the side walls, pulling me onto his lap. Before I could catch my breath, he slipped his hand under my hair and pulled me into him, smothering me with his kiss.

"Thomas," I gasped, pulling away. "I have to—"

He shook his head quickly and pulled me in again. My heart pounded. My fingers touched his face, his neck, grasped his shoulders. His hands ran down my back, over my stomach, grazed my breasts, and then returned to my face. I was overcome with heat and longing. I pressed myself closer and closer to him, knowing all the while that we could be caught at any moment, that I was making myself later and later for my meeting, that this was very, very wrong.

"This is all I think about," Thomas said breathlessly, breaking away for the slightest second.

"Me too," I said. I struggled to catch my breath. "But I have to go."

"When I saw you come around the corner I thought I was seeing things," he said, searching my eyes. "But you were really there."

I giggled. "Yeah. I really was," I said. "But I do have to go."

Thomas kissed me again and I could feel his desperation to keep me there. Still, somehow, I slid away, groping for my bag on the damp stone floor.

"We have to do this again," Thomas said, gazing up at me, his chest heaving up and down.

"Yeah," I replied. "We most definitely do."

THE FEAR

"Miss Brennan, when we first met and I told you I would be keeping a close eye on you, did it sound like I was making a joke?"

I tried to stop smiling. I really did. But after that encounter with Thomas, it was impossible.

"No."

"Well then, I assume you were unaware that I receive weekly reports from every one of your teachers," she said, the jowls shaking. They grazed the high collar of her silk purple shirt, leaving a nasty stain of makeup residue behind.

"Yes." I blinked and shifted in my seat, pressing my lips together. Serious. This was serious. "I mean, I didn't know that. No."

Ms. Naylor narrowed her eyes at me. She clucked her tongue as she lifted a sheet of paper from her desk toward the dim light. "Unsatisfactory," she read. She picked up another sheet, holding it the same way. "Minimal effort shown." Another. "Little to no preparation for class and quizzes."

I grew warmer with each comment she read and finally the

giddiness was tempered. I tried to discern which teacher had said what, and therefore whom I now hated the most. Unfortunately, when I thought about it, I realized that any one of them could have said any of these things. They were all right. I had turned out to be an abysmal student.

"One more round of grades like this and you will be put on academic probation. Your scholarship will be reassessed and the Board of Directors might begin to wonder if it made a mistake in admitting you," she said, lifting her chin imperiously. "Believe me when I tell you that the Board of Directors does not appreciate being shown that it has made a mistake."

It was weird the way she referred to the board as an "it" instead of a "they." Grammatically correct, maybe, but it made me think of a supercomputer behind a green curtain handing down verdicts from on high. It was effective, though. I officially had the fear.

"Now, what are we going to do about this, Miss Brennan?" Naylor asked, laying the papers down and lacing her bulbous fingers together on top of them.

I swallowed hard. "Study harder?" I suggested.

She stared as if waiting for me to tell her this was a joke.

"*I* suggest you stop spending so much time socializing with the women of Billings House and get yourself to the library," she said finally. My jaw dropped. Her lips twitched and I could tell she was pleased with herself for shocking me. She tapped her fingertip to her temple near the corner of her heavily made-up eye. "I told you I would be watching. You should start taking both me and your education more seriously."

Disturbing. Very disturbing.

"If you are no longer a student at Easton, then you won't have your new friends or that Thomas Pearson to spend time with anymore, will you?"

Oh, God. Had she seen us? Why was she looking at me that way?

"Now, are you going to start taking your schooling more seriously?" she asked, her eyes gleaming in triumph.

"I . . . I will," I said, trying to figure out where the school had hidden the secret surveillance cameras. Other than at morning services, I had never seen Ms. Naylor outside her cave. How did she know whom I was hanging out with?

"Very well, then. You're excused."

I scrambled out of my seat and her office, feeling her eyes on the back of my neck. Once outside, I took a deep breath and considered everything she had said. She may have been creepy and potentially voyeuristic, but the woman had a point. If I didn't pull my grades up I was going to be booted, and then I wouldn't have the Billings Girls *or* Thomas to distract me anymore. I would be on a Greyhound back to Croton before you could say "big fat failure."

RESIDENT GENIUS

Outside it was a warm, sunny day, and on my way to lunch I saw Noelle, Ariana, Taylor, and Kiran all kicked out on the grass in the quad, soaking up the rays. Kiran's shirt was pulled up to expose her stomach and her face was tipped toward the sky. Noelle was propped up on her elbows, debating something with Taylor, who picked at the grass. Ariana lay with her back on the ground and her feet up on a bench, her book lifted in front of her face. She had moved on from *Anna Karenina* and was now reading *The Brothers Karamazov*.

The other students trailed by the Billings Girls on their way to the cafeteria, casting sidelong glances in their direction. During the school day, we weren't supposed to lounge anywhere unless we were sick, and then it was to the infirmary with us. I heaved a sigh as I walked by them.

"Problem, glass-licker?" Noelle asked.

I paused, uncertain, and hovered a few feet away, clasping the strap on my bag with both hands. It had been a long time since any one of these girls had acknowledged me outside the cafeteria. "No. I'm fine," I said.

"No, you're not. You just came from Ms. Naylor's office," Ariana said, never taking her eyes off her book. How did she *know* that? She turned the page lazily and continued reading.

Kiran slid her designer sunglasses down and looked at me over the top. "Oh, yeah. She's got that look."

"What look?" I asked.

"That 'I just got my first grades at Easton and now I'm suicidal' look," Noelle said, casually crossing her legs at the ankles.

Taylor sucked air through her teeth. "That bad, huh?"

Sometimes I forgot how much these girls knew about this place. How integrated they were into the inner workings of Easton. A few years here and they knew everything that was going on. I wondered if I would ever have that kind of Easton wisdom. I wondered if I would even be here long enough to find out what next week's Friday dinner special would be.

"I can handle it," I said.

"Bullshit," Noelle replied. "You look like the stick you just peed on turned blue. Get Taylor to help you."

Taylor's eyes brightened and she sat up. "I'll *totally* help you."

"Really?" I asked. I couldn't believe the Billings Girls were actually offering their aid. They hadn't forced me to run any overly heinous errands for them in days, either. Was it possible that the torture was over? Maybe they were finally accepting me.

"She helps all of us," Noelle said, closing her eyes as she tilted her face toward the sun. "Why do you think we hang out with her?"

Taylor's face dropped. Clearly this comment hit a little too close to home.

"Noelle," Ariana said in a scolding way.

Noelle's eyes widened and she sat up again. "What? She knows I'm kidding," she said. "Taylor, you do know I'm kidding?"

Taylor managed to nod, but I could tell she was totally thrown.

"Don't you have a ton of your own work to do?" I asked her.

Before Taylor could answer, Noelle scoffed. "Please. She's already done all her coursework for the semester. Plus mine," she added under her breath.

Kiran snickered and I wondered if this was actually true. For some reason, it wouldn't have surprised me. Maybe this really *was* why Noelle kept Taylor around. It would explain why a girl of such amorphous attitude tolerated someone so steadfastly sweet.

"Really. It's no problem," Taylor told me.

"You're so lazy, Lange," Kiran said to Noelle, yawning. She turned over onto her stomach, readjusting her shirt for maximum back exposure. There was a black tattoo on the small of her back; it looked like an Egyptian sphinx. I wanted to ask her about it, but Noelle cut me off.

"Look who's talking. I think your ass has grown exponentially since we got here," Noelle said.

"I'm impressed you know the word 'exponentially,' " Kiran shot back with a smirk.

"Girls," Ariana said, shaking her head.

Noelle sighed and picked up her bag, pushing herself from the ground. "You should let her help you, glass-licker," she said as everyone else scrambled to their feet, following her lead as always.

"She may look and act like a dumb blonde, but she's almost freak-ishly smart."

Taylor turned pink, but said nothing. She smiled at me encour-agingly, hugging her books to her chest.

"Okay," I said finally. "If you really don't mind."

"Cool! When do you want to meet?"

She seemed inordinately psyched about helping me study, but it made me feel ten times better. And even better, the Billings Girls were extending a hand of friendship, and that hand could very well help me get my grades up and keep me here at Easton. This day was turning right around.

INTENSE

The next few days were a flurry of studying, soccer, and secret make-out sessions with Thomas. Every time I saw him he would find some way to touch me or tickle me or kiss me. We made out behind the landscaper's cottage after breakfast one morning. On my way back from practice on a sunny afternoon he pulled me into the baseball dugout where I let him slide his hands under my shirt and under my bra for the first time, shaking with nerves and paranoia all the while.

But mostly we met up in our own secret place, inside the entryway to Gwendolyn Hall. There we were still on edge, but felt safer than anywhere else. I would sit on Thomas's lap or he would lay me back on his jacket and we would touch and kiss and explore each other until the last possible second. Until we had to run off to class or dorm meetings or practices.

Still, each one of these encounters was rushed and panicked, with the two of us constantly listening for footfalls and checking over our shoulders for prying eyes. All of which made each meeting that much more exhilarating, made me that much more desperate to go further each time. Before we were caught. Before we were exposed.

One afternoon, I rushed from lunch to meet up with Thomas at Gwendolyn as planned, and was confused when I saw him walking toward me on the quad. His face was wan and his expression distracted, his eyes darting from face to face. I figured he was looking for me and lifted my hand to get his attention, but he blew right by me.

"Thomas?"

He stopped and turned around. Every movement was sharp and deliberate, his casual demeanor gone.

"What's wrong?"

"I can't talk right now," he said.

"But I thought we—"

"I can't," he repeated firmly. Then he glanced around and took a couple steps closer to me. He lowered his voice. "You haven't seen my phone, have you?"

"Your cell? No. Why?" I asked, baffled.

"What the hell could I have done with it?" he blurted, turning away. He covered his mouth with both hands set in a steeple and looked across the campus, racking his brain. "I have to find it," he said, starting off again.

"I'll help you," I said, scurrying after him.

"No."

His response was so harsh it made me stop in my tracks. Thomas saw my face and sighed. "This is my problem. Don't worry about it," he said. "Just go to class and I'll . . . catch up with you later."

I tried not to let the depth of my disappointment show in my eyes. I had been looking forward to hooking up with him all morning. But I could tell that he was clearly wigged about losing his phone. I wasn't about to guilt him over it.

Besides, waiting would just make our next meeting that much more intense. I could cope with that.

"I hope you find it," I said as he walked away.

He didn't even seem to hear me.

The entire Croton Municipal Library could have fit in the foyer of the Easton Library. Apparently Mitchell Easton, who founded the school with his brother Micah back in the day, was a huge bibliophile. He had traveled around the world gathering original texts to fill the shelves of his beloved library, the construction of which he had overseen himself. Or so I had read on the bronze plaque near the front door while I waited for Taylor to show up for our first study session that night. Upon arriving fifteen minutes late, Taylor had apologized, explaining that she had been on the phone with her little sister, pep-talking her for musical auditions at her school back in Indiana. Until that moment, I had no idea Taylor was from the Midwest and now I felt a definite kinship with her. I was not the only person around here who had not grown up in New York, Boston, Chicago, or L.A.

"Mr. Barber likes to think he has us all shaking in our shoes, but last year I figured out his pattern," she whispered to me across the wide, gleaming, oak table we had commandeered in the stacks. The place was deathly quiet, the only sound the whirring of a far-off copy machine somewhere near the back wall.

"His pattern?" I whispered, leaning forward.

Taylor smiled mischievously and I realized she was in her element. She was a lot more confident, playful, and talkative here among the books than she was among her friends.

"Everyone thinks his weekly quizzes are killers, but I guarantee you I can predict almost every question he asks," Taylor said, opening my history book to chapter six and turning it toward me on the table. "He takes all his questions from the third sentences of paragraphs within the required reading." She used her pencil's eraser as a pointer. "Here. 'On July 12, 1812, General Hull and his troops crossed into Canada at Sandwich.'" She read upside down faster than I did right side up. "That's the third sentence of a paragraph. You can forget about everything else after that. Just memorize that information and you'll be fine."

"No way," I said, sliding the book toward me.

"Trust me. If you don't get at least a ninety-two on his next quiz, you can take it out on me," she said.

I smiled and opened up my notebook so I could start making lists. I felt as if someone had just handed me a limit-free charge card. That's how excited I was to show Mr. Barber up.

"I think I might love you," I told Taylor.

She laughed and was clearly pleased. "Get all that info down and then we'll talk about how to impress Miss Krantz," Taylor said, pulling a romance novel out of her bag. "Woman has a thing for oral reports about food. I have no idea why. I don't think she's eaten a real meal since the Clinton administration."

I laughed.

"Aren't you going to study?" I asked, eyeing her well-worn book.

"Remember what Noelle said about me having done the whole semester's work?" she said.

I nodded.

"She wasn't kidding."

Damn.

I opened my notebook and was about to get to work when Taylor's cell phone vibrated on the table. She glanced at it and rolled her eyes.

"It's for you," she said.

My brow creased, but I took the phone. The text message read: "smarter yet glasslicker?"

I snorted a laugh. I put my pen down and texted back "almost."

The moment I placed the phone down, it vibrated again. Taylor shot it an irritated look. This time the text read: "y dont u have ur own phone? r u a loser?'

I flushed and texted back "not allowed." More like "have no money." But she didn't need to know that.

The response was almost instantaneous: "have 2 fx that."

Whatever that meant. I placed the phone down and it vibrated again. Taylor clucked her tongue and picked it up. She texted back furiously.

"What did you say?" I asked, hoping that whatever it was wouldn't get Noelle mad at me.

"I just reminded her that if we didn't get your grades up, they'd send you home. And she doesn't want that to happen."

Really? Well, that was . . . interesting. Hard to believe that Noelle could possibly care whether I was here or not, but good to hear.

I smiled, flattered and somewhat relieved. But a second later, the phone vibrated again. I grabbed it playfully before Taylor could get to it, then was appalled at my own audacity. This wasn't my phone, and Noelle might be writing something private to Taylor. I was about to hand it back when I saw the text was not from Noelle. It was from Thomas. Apparently he had found his phone. My heart sunk. Why was Thomas texting Taylor? But in the next second I realized that this message, too, was for me.

"New grl: ketlar common room. 8pm. b there." An invite to the guys' dorm. From Thomas. This day just kept getting more and more interesting. Taylor must have noticed my elated expression because she grabbed the phone out of my hand. She glanced at the message, scoffed, and turned off the phone.

"You can play with your boyfriend when you're done with your work," she said in a faux-mom tone.

I snorted a laugh. She smiled. I could think about Noelle and her plans later. If I didn't do this work now, I might never get the chance to find out what they were.

Of course, who knew if that would be a good thing or a bad thing?

KETLAR HOUSE

When I arrived at Ketlar that night, Thomas took my hand and led me right through the common room and down the hallway toward his dorm room. He opened the door and stood there, waiting for me to go in. Beyond the threshold, I saw two beds made with dark spreads. One side of the room was messy and covered with art supplies, an easel standing in the corner. The other side was almost pathologically neat with a variety of electronics glowing and whirring in the darkness. The only light came from a small, green desk lamp.

"What're we doing?" I asked, my pulse racing with both trepidation and excitement.

"Go in," Thomas said.

I hesitated. This was so very against the rules.

"Go in," Thomas repeated, this time a touch more firmly. My pulse skipped and prodded me over the threshold. Thomas closed the door behind us and we were alone. In his room. I was alone in a boy's dorm room with the door closed.

"What are we doing?' I said again.

"I'm sorry I missed today," he said, taking my hand and kissing it. "I wanted to make it up to you."

My heart thumped, but I turned away. He wasn't actually suggesting we hook up here. Now. In his room. A girl could get expelled for this type of thing. I picked up his cell from his desk, stalling for time.

"I see you found this," I said. "Where was it?"

Just then, another cell phone bleeped. I glanced at Josh's side of the room, but then Thomas whipped a second phone out of his pocket.

"Hang on," he told me. He flipped the phone open and turned away from me. "Pearson."

I stared down at the phone in my hand. He had two? Why did he have two? Wasn't *one* extravagant enough? And if it was always with you, you would never need another.

"No. Yeah. That's fine," Thomas said quickly into the phone. "I'll be there."

Then he snapped the phone closed and sighed. "Sorry," he said, tucking the second cell into the pocket of his suede jacket, which hung off his closet door. "That was Lawrence and Trina."

I raised my eyebrows at him.

"The elder regents," he explained. "They're the only ones that have that number."

"Because . . . ?"

"They pay for it. That was why I freaked when I lost it. I had to get a new one activated before they found out. My parents already think I'm irresponsible enough."

Ah. So it was this other, parental phone that had gone missing. He leaned over and plucked the first cell from my fingers. "This one *I* pay for. This is the number all the important people get."

He reached by me and placed it back on the desk. He was inches away. "I don't need my parents checking out my bill and prying into my life," he said, looking deep into my eyes. "It's just easier this way."

I felt sorry for him. That he had to go so far to separate himself from these people who were supposed to love him. Of course, I had to move hundreds of miles away for the same reason.

"Have you decided what to do? About parents' weekend?" I asked, looking down at my fingers.

He took a deep breath and blew it out. "No. You?"

My heart hurt whenever I thought about my father. He had mentioned it on the phone once or twice since he'd first brought it up. That he'd received an invitation. That they were excited about it. Personally, I couldn't imagine my mother being excited about anything, let alone anything that had to do with me. But the guilt whenever I thought about telling him to stay away was overwhelming.

"No," I admitted.

"You know what? I don't want to talk about this," Thomas said lightly. "I asked you here because I knew you'd had a long day and I thought I'd help you destress."

He smiled and stepped behind me. Slowly he slid my jacket off and let it fall to the ground. My breath caught in my throat as he placed his hands on my shoulders. Softly, he touched my neck with his lips and my eyes fluttered closed. A thrill of anticipation rushed through me. There was so much wrong with this that it made me want to be there even more.

Thomas tugged slightly on my shoulder and I turned around. We kissed deeply—slowly at first. I trembled as I grasped at the back of his shirt, holding on. I was all nerves and excitement and curiosity and I just wanted to keep touching him. He held me tightly in his arms and pulled me closer and closer into him until I heard a noise in the hallway and jumped away.

He stepped forward and took my hand, tugging me toward the neat-as-a-pin bed. "It's okay," he said. "No one's coming down here. I promise."

"How do you know?" I asked, my heart pounding in my throat.

"I have ways," Thomas replied.

He pulled me down on his bed and my leg hooked over his. He slid his hands underneath my hair and pulled me to him. His kiss was urgent. Almost violent. And I knew for sure what he wanted. Why I was there.

He slid his hands under my shirt and my breath caught in anticipation. But to my surprise, his palms stopped on my stomach. He pulled back and looked into my eyes.

"You know I love you, right?" he whispered.

I was so shocked I almost laughed.

"You don't have to say that," I said.

Briefly, anger flashed through his eyes. "I'm not lying. I love you. I wouldn't be doing this if I didn't."

Yeah, right.

Then I saw the sincerity in his eyes, and felt guilty for my disloyal thoughts. Okay. Did he want me to tell him I loved him back? *Did* I love him back? I had no idea. Should I say it if I wasn't sure? Would he flip out if I didn't?

"I—"

"Don't say anything," Thomas said. "It's okay. I just want to be with you."

I swallowed hard. In that moment I knew. I knew that I was going to give him what he wanted. I was going to give him everything.

"Okay," I said.

And he smiled and kissed me, leaning me slowly backward onto his bed.

A GIFT

It was done. My virginity. Officially gone. Lost. Given away. As I walked up the hill to soccer practice the next day, I tried to wrap my brain around it. Tried to decide how I felt about it. In all my life I had never thought that I would be a person who just let it happen. I always thought there would be build-up, conversations, long, agonizing decisions. But instead, I had just gone with it. I had just made the decision in the moment and let it happen. In a way, I was proud of myself that I'd been so bold. But on the other hand, I knew it was perhaps not the wisest move in the world. Letting something that big just happen was very unlike me.

But whenever I thought of Thomas's hands, his kiss, his scent, I smiled and shivered and wished I was with him again. Alone. In his room in the dark. And that was all I needed to make any misgivings fade to the background. Thomas and I had been together. He was my first. There was no going back now.

And I liked that idea.

Of course, there were a million things to consider now. Should I get birth control? Could I be the kind of girl who carried condoms around in her backpack? And where the hell would one even get that kind of thing in this cloistered place?

"What's eating you, glass-licker?" Noelle asked, jogging to catch up with me.

I flinched, feeling as if I had just been caught. An answer. An answer. I needed an answer.

"It's parents' weekend," I said.

Noelle laughed. "Thomas rubbing off on you?"

I flushed, thinking of Thomas's room. Of his body. Of his skin against mine.

"No. It's not that." I looked up the hill at our teammates who were a good ten yards ahead, chatting and laughing. "I'm not looking forward to it either. It has nothing to do with him."

"Oh. Trouble at home?" she asked facetiously, sticking out her bottom lip.

"Thanks a lot," I said, with a little more venom than I intended.

Noelle's eyes lit with surprise. "Look. If you don't want your parents here, you don't have to have them here. It's your life. You don't owe them anything."

She was wrong. I owed my father everything. But I knew he wasn't coming here without my mother. He clung to the idea that we could be a normal, happy family. Besides, she would grumble about the expense and inconvenience of taking the trip, but the fit she would throw if he tried to come without her would be level five all the way—even though she didn't actually want to be here. The depth of my mother's psychosis was staggering.

"I just don't know how I would tell him . . . ," I said, thinking aloud, then flushing. Noelle looked at me expectantly. "Never mind."

Another thing I wasn't ready to do with Noelle was trust her with my secrets.

We reached the top of the hill and already most of our teammates were running drills on the field. Noelle dropped her bag at her feet. She swung her thick hair behind her shoulders and reached back to gather it up into a ponytail.

"If you want me to be there when you make the call, I will," Noelle offered. "I'm usually good at bringing out the ass-kicker in people."

My incredulousness must have shown, because she smirked.

"Don't give me that," she said. "I mean, if we daughters of fucked-up families can't stick together, than where the hell will we be?"

I smiled. I had no idea what was screwed up about her family, but it made me feel better. If she was going to start telling me little bits about herself, maybe I could start to do the same. Maybe. Sometime.

"Oh. I almost forgot." She crouched and reached into the side pocket on her bag. She pulled out a small, blue cell phone and held it up in the palm of her hand. "For you."

"What?" I said, picking up the phone. On the screen were the words "Glass-licker's Phone."

No one had ever given me anything this expensive. Or this extravagant. Even if it did say "Glass-licker" instead of "Reed."

"You're kidding me," I said.

"Do I *look* like I'm kidding?" she replied.

My mouth was hanging open. "There's no way I can accept this."

"You already have," she said with a shrug.

"But what about the . . .uh . . ."

"The bill? Taken care of. I don't give people presents they have to pay for."

"Noelle—"

She stood and hoisted her bag. "Look, we can't have you being unavailable, can we?" she said, walking backward toward the field.

I blinked. The foreboding was back. Was this part of whatever plan Noelle had in store for me? The plan Taylor almost mistakenly divulged? "What do you mean?"

"Who knows? There may be some kind of glass-licking emergency," she said teasingly.

"Lange! Brennan! Get your butts out here!" Coach shouted, waving her arm at us.

Noelle grinned at me, then turned and strolled at her own leisurely pace toward the field.

ANGER

When Noelle arrived at my room that night, she spent ten minutes blatantly looking around, picking up books, studying posters, squinting at pictures. I wouldn't have been surprised if she had started opening drawers. And I probably would have let her. Privacy was not an issue. All I could think about as she conducted her search was whether or not everything would meet with her approval. Finally she sat down on Constance's bed and regarded me with an open expression.

"Let's do this," she said.

I nodded and sat across from her. The cell phone was slippery from my palm sweat. Just dialing on the tiny buttons was difficult. My father answered on the second ring, sounding alert and paranoid. He always sounded this way when he answered the phone.

"Hello?"

"Hi, Dad. It's me."

"Reed! Hi, kiddo!" His voice completely changed and the rush of guilt was overwhelming. He sounded excited. Happy even. I glanced helplessly at Noelle. She gave me a stern look.

"To what do I owe the pleasure?" he asked.

"Actually, it's about parents' weekend," I said.

I was going to die from this pain. I really was. I squirmed and clutched at my bedspread.

"Your mother and I are so looking forward to it," he said.

Oh, God. Come on!

"Tell him!" Noelle whispered, kicking my foot.

I shot her a look of death. If I hadn't been so overwrought already, that never would have happened. She simply stared back, urging me on.

"Well, that's the thing," I said. I squeezed my eyes shut. "I don't think you should come."

A laugh. Then a pause. "What? Why?"

Even in my guilt, I rolled my eyes. "You *know* why, Dad."

"Reed, your mother *wants* to come," he said. "She even bought a new outfit."

I swallowed hard. The outfit was not for me. I knew the way her mind worked. She was all about appearances. She wanted the other parents to think she belonged. But her nature would win out over her facade. There was no way she would get through the weekend without showing her true colors—without spewing them all over me. Just the mental picture was all I needed to go on.

"It doesn't matter, Dad. I don't want her here," I said.

"Now, Reed—"

"I'm not going to change my mind," I told him, earning a resolute nod from Noelle. "She'll ruin everything. We both know it. Besides, think of all the money you'll save—"

I glanced at Noelle. Saw her register this. I had just shown her my cards. No going back now.

"Oh, Reed. It's not about the money," my father said. "Don't do this—"

"I'm sorry, Dad," I said, ready to burst into tears for any number of reasons. "I don't want you to come and I'm not gonna change my mind."

There was a long pause. I imagined him in the kitchen, lowering his heavy frame onto one of the wooden chairs around the table. His slumped shoulders. His hand on his face. I was going to cry at any second.

"What am I going to tell your mother?" he said finally. "She's been in so much pain lately. . . ."

And there it was. What it was all about. Her. How she would feel. How she would react. The terror and guilt she would rain down on all of us when she was disappointed. I was so sick of it. So sick of living in fear of her. The woman even had my father quaking in his boots.

"Tell her to call *me*," I said sharply. "If that's what she wants."

"Reed. I was so looking forward to it," he said. "To seeing you."

My heart clenched. Not for the first time, I wished it were just my dad. That would make life so much easier. Maybe if I could just have *him* come. Maybe if there was a way . . .

I felt myself start to crumble and I glanced at Noelle. She must have seen the weakness in my eyes because hers grew dark.

"Don't you cave," she said through her teeth. "Do not cave."

And that was all I needed. I couldn't crumble in front of her.

"I'm sorry, Dad," I said honestly. "I can't do it."

"I wish you didn't have so much anger," he said, sounding sad and resigned.

You try growing up in that household and coming out all rainbows and unicorns.

"Yeah. Me too," I said.

Noelle looked confused. I took a deep breath. This had gone on long enough. I needed to get off the phone. I needed to get off and hit something. "I have to go now, Dad. We have to go to dinner."

"Okay. Reed, if you change your mind . . . ," he said hopefully. So hopefully it killed.

"Yeah, Dad. I know. I'll talk to you soon."

I hung up before he could even say good-bye.

"Nice work, glass-licker," Noelle said, slapping me on the shoulder.

"Would you *please* stop calling me that?" I blurted.

Surprised anger flashed across her face and for a split second I thought she was going to explode. But then she smiled.

"All you had to do was ask."

CLARITY

I split off from Noelle on the way to dinner, hoping to find Thomas before everyone got to the table. After my phone call with my father I was a jumble of warring emotions. At turns I was proud of myself, then guilty, then free, then miserable. I wanted to both laugh and burst into tears. I needed to talk to Thomas. I needed to talk to someone who would understand.

The weather had changed as if to match my mood. A light drizzle had started to fall just before we left Bradwell, matched with a chilly wind. I pulled my denim jacket tighter around me as I approached the cafeteria. Fall was definitely here. Students rushed by me, hustling to get inside before the sky opened up. When I saw Thomas standing outside the double doors I felt instantly relieved. He was, as always, surrounded by random students, some of whom I now knew and some of whom I had only seen around. Easton was small enough that by this time I had seen everyone around. Thomas caught my eye, said a few words to his entourage, and they all dispersed quickly. Sometimes I thought I was dating not only the most popular guy in school, but also the most powerful. People always seemed to listen and act on every word he said.

"Hey," he said, wrapping his warm arms around me.

I sunk into him, breathing in his clean scent. So much better.

"Hey," I replied. "So, I did it."

"Did what?" he asked. He leaned back slightly to look into my eyes.

"I told my parents not to come." Even as I said it, my heart clenched.

Thomas's face lit up in a way I had never seen before. For the first time, I could clearly see what he had looked like as a little boy. A little boy who had just been given a shiny new bike. Or in Thomas's case, perhaps a helicopter.

"This is perfect!" he said. "Now you can come to lunch with me and my parents."

I looked at him, confused. "Since when are you so psyched about lunch with your parents?" Part of me had thought that since I had stood up to my dad, maybe he would be able to do the same. Apparently he wasn't so inclined or inspired.

"Since you became available," he replied, settling back into his cool demeanor. "They're dying to meet you. And when they're dying to meet someone, they're usually on their best behavior."

A bunch of girls from my floor walked by us in a clump, chatting loudly as they slipped into the cafeteria.

"Why are they dying to meet me?" I asked.

"I told them about you and they love that I have an actual

girlfriend," he said with a small smile. "Any sign of stability in my life sends them into ecstatic convulsions."

"Wow. So, have you never had a girlfriend before?" I asked.

"Not one worth telling them about," he replied. I flushed with pleasure as he wrapped his arms around my waist and pulled me closer to him. "So come. Please? It'll make everything *so* much easier."

I was flattered. Flattered and honored and just happy. Thomas wanted me to meet his parents. He practically needed me to. All the guilt I had been feeling over my own family was pushed aside. Noelle was right. This was my life now.

"Okay," I said finally.

"Really?"

"Are you kidding?" I said with a playful smile. "Count me in. I can not *wait* to meet Lawrence and Trina."

NEW TASK

I was just dozing off when my cell phone beeped. I jumped up, heart in my throat. I glanced at the digital clock on Constance's desk: 12:01 a.m. Who the hell was texting me at 12:01? It beeped again and I scrambled through my bag for it, glancing over at Constance as I blindly searched. Her chest rose and fell in its normal rhythm without so much as a flinch. A sleep that deep could not be safe. But at least it was good for me.

The screen of my cell was alight with a text message. I lost all breath when I saw the words.

MEET BEHIND BILLINGS. U HAVE 3 MINS.

What the?

Okay. Apparently the slave portion of my relationship with the Billings Girls was *not* over.

Unfortunately, I didn't have time to think. I jumped up, threw a sweatshirt on over my pajama pants, and jammed my bare feet into sneakers. I felt loud and awkward and clumsy as I tiptoed out of the room and closed the door behind me. I bypassed the elevator—which had a *ping!* that could wake the dead and was right next to Miss Ling's room on the first floor—and headed for the stairs. My heart was in my throat all the way down the five flights and into the lobby. I held on to the heavy back door to Bradwell until it finally clicked closed, expecting at every second for Miss Ling to appear, fearing that I'd tripped some silent alarm. But nothing happened.

Thank God.

Outside, the air chilled my bones and the sky was as black as death. No moon. No stars. I tripped myself twice on the short run across to Billings and prayed the girls weren't watching me fumbling and stumbling. About ten seconds later I found myself standing near the back wall of Billings, facing Noelle, Ariana, Kiran, and Taylor. I gasped for breath.

"You were almost late," Kiran said, her glossy lips pursed.

"Sorry," I replied, trying to stand up straight.

"We need you to do something for us," Noelle said.

Shocker. I didn't actually think I was here for an appreciation party.

"What?" I asked.

"Ariana has a physics test tomorrow," Taylor said. "We need you to get it for her."

The ground dropped out from underneath me. *"What?"*

"I didn't have time to study," Ariana said blithely.

"And I didn't have time to tutor her," Taylor said.

I stared at her. Was this really the same girl who helped me so selflessly with my work? I had thought she was kind. Normal even. Now she was staring me down with the rest of them asking me to, what? Break into a teacher's office?

"Don't look so freaked," Noelle said. "Dramble's office is on the first floor of Hell Hall. It's a piece of cake."

"If it's such a piece of cake, why aren't you doing it?" I asked. Then immediately regretted it.

"Excuse me?" Kiran said, her brow creased in disbelief.

"I thought you'd want to help me, but if you'd rather I fail . . . " Ariana said, playing the martyr.

"No. It's fine," I said, my throat dry. "How do I do it?"

"You're a smart kid," Noelle said, patting me on the shoulder. "You can figure it out."

They weren't even going to give me a hint? What the hell kind of people were they?

"Now go," Noelle said. "If you're not back here in fifteen minutes, we'll be forced to report you to security."

One look in her eye told me she was not kidding.

"Go," she said again.

I thought about what they were asking me to do. I thought about what would happen if I got caught. I thought about my life back home and my life here and how everything I had ever wanted would be within my grasp, but only so long as I was connected to the Billings Girls.

Of course, I did all this thinking in two seconds flat. Then I turned around and ran.

SMOOTH CRIMINAL

One single light flickered above the arched entryway to Hell Hall. It was a thick wooden door with one long, pebbled-glass window in the center. I looked around and took the steps to the door two at a time, hoping for a miracle. One tug on the wrought-iron handle told me I had no such luck. The place was locked up tight.

"Shit," I said under my breath.

Back down the stairs, I raced into the darkness along the side of the building and felt slightly safer. At least I was no longer right out in the open for all the world to see and expel. But as I inspected the cold stone walls I realized how very screwed I was. The first floor windows were set high above my head. I slid between two azalea bushes and stood on my toes, reaching for one of the windows. My fingertips just grazed the lower sill. There was absolutely no way I could get up there, even if one of them happened to be unlocked.

How in God's name could anyone classify this mission as cake? This was impossible.

I glanced at my watch. Already four minutes had gone by since I left the Billings Girls. Were they really going to call security on me? If they did, I was out on my ass.

These could very well be my last moments at Easton.

No. There had to be another way in. There had to be. All I had to do was find it. And use it to get in. And find my way to Dramble's office in the pitch black dark and . . .

I better get going.

I stepped backward and tripped over a spigot in the ground. My palm caught on a rough patch of wall as I went down and I flinched in pain. I was about to shove myself up again when I saw it. A small window set low in the ground. It was about a foot and a half tall and four feet wide and looked as if it were made of two sliding panes of glass. My heart took a hopeful leap. Basement windows. Of course. I had seen Kiran and her Dreck boy use one before. Apparently this was Easton's weak link, probably one of those things everyone knew about at this school. At least if they had been here more than a few weeks.

I crawled over the cold dirt toward the window, the branches of the bushes that disguised them scratching at my face. I placed my hand flat against the glass, said a quick prayer, and tried to slide the pane aside. Nothing happened. I whimpered and tried again. Nothing. I dug my fingernails between the edge of the glass and the window frame and pulled with all my might, holding my breath.

Two seconds later I fell backward, nearly ripping three of my fingernails free. The pain was excruciating.

Screw them. Screw them and their test. Let Ariana fail. Let her see what it's like.

But even as I thought it I knew I would never let them down. I held on to my fingers and bit back the tears. I had to keep trying.

Three feet away was another window. Once again I pressed my hand against it, held my breath, and closed my eyes. I pushed. And the window slid open.

Yes! I was saved.

I shoved my head inside the cool dankness of a basement storage room. Desks and chairs were stacked all around the perimeter and beneath the window was a long, metal desk. I turned around and went through backward. The metal slider rail of the window cut into my legs, then my stomach as I shimmied through, but I ignored the pain. I dangled for a second, then dropped onto the desk with a bang that reverberated throughout the world. I closed my eyes and nearly burst into tears. There was no way that had gone unnoticed.

Apparently I was unfit for a life of crime.

But it didn't matter. I had to go. Somewhere on the first floor was Mr. Dramble's office. I still had to find it, then find the test, then get the hell out of there and back to Billings.

I raced to the door and whipped it open, not even checking to see if there was anyone around. If they were, they were already on their way thanks to my spectacularly unstealthy entrance. May as well get as far as I could.

I found the stairwell at the back of the building and ran up to the first floor. The only light came from a red exit sign that cast the walls in a bloodlike hue. I ran along, checking the names on the brass plates next to each wood-and-glass door.

Ms. Johnson. Mr. Carter. Mr. Cross.

And then, finally, at the end of the hall, I found it. Mr. Dramble.

I grasped the handle and turned. It was, mercifully, unlocked. Perhaps, like the dorms, none of the teacher's rooms were ever locked. There was, after all, an honor code around here. Perhaps the brass at Easton felt that was enough to keep people like me out.

Oh, well.

I fumbled through the office, slammed my foot into a chair, and eventually groped my way to the desk. As my eyes adjusted, I found a desk light and flicked it on. Dangerous, I know, but I was completely unfamiliar with my surroundings. Unless I wanted to break something or injure myself, I needed light. Dramble's computer was on a low cart next to his desk. I pressed the on button and held my breath as the computer whirred to life. It took forever to boot up and I wished I had grabbed a watch on my way out. I had no idea how much time I was wasting here. Five minutes? Ten? It felt like five hours.

Finally the desktop appeared. A picture of a miniature schnauzer in the center. Various folder icons were lined up on the right side. My breath caught when I saw that one was marked "Senior Physics."

Hands trembling, I grabbed the mouse and double-clicked the folder. There were at least two dozen files named "quiz_9_21," "quiz 9_28" and "exam_1," "exam_2." And on and on. Which exam was it? Had they already taken one or was this their first? *Crap.* I would just have to print out a few.

I opened the first four exam files and sent them to the printer. When it creaked to life, I died a slow death. The printer was ancient and louder than an A-bomb. When it started printing, I actually squeezed out a tear of desperation. One page an hour, approximately.

As each page printed, I snatched it from the printer. My feet tapped. My hands quaked. My heart was executing an erratic beat that had to be unhealthy. Finally, finally, the last page came through. I lunged at the computer and shut it down; then, having no clue if the security detail was already in the building looking for me, I bolted.

In the hallway I paused for a millisecond. I listened for footsteps and heard nothing.

Maybe luck *was* on my side.

Knowing there was absolutely no way I could climb up the basement wall and back out through that tiny window, I headed for the front door. I ran as fast as I could down the hallway, rounded a corner, and skidded into the entryway hall. I was about to run for the door when everything dropped out from under me and I fell to the floor in horror.

There was a face in the window.

AN INVITATION

I heard the cackle of a laugh and slowly looked up. It was Noelle. Noelle was standing just outside the door.

"Reed Brennan! Come on out!" she sang quietly.

Shaking and cursing under my breath, I pushed myself to my feet and staggered for the door. As I shoved it open, Noelle, Ariana, Kiran, and Taylor all moved aside. Noelle's face had been distorted by the pebbling in the window, but if I hadn't been in such a panic and if I'd had a second longer to take her in, I would have realized it was her. I felt like a total idiot. I had fallen to the floor right in front of her.

She grabbed my hand and pulled me, still laughing, into the shadows, the rest of the girls at our heels. I started to seethe.

"You should have seen your face," Noelle whispered mirthfully once we were a safe distance from all buildings housing any adults.

"Sorry I missed it," I said, whipping the test out and handing it to Ariana. "Here. Enjoy."

"Oh! She's upset!" Kiran teased.

"Calm down, Reed. It was just a joke," Taylor said.

"Great. Funny. Can I go to bed now?" I asked.

Noelle paused. Her eyes darkened. "You keep up that attitude and you won't get what you have coming to you."

My heart skipped a distressed, curious beat. "What do you mean?"

"Well, we were going to have you over tomorrow if you got Ariana the test," Kiran said. "But if you're not interested . . ."

Have me over? As in over to Billings? As in me *inside* Billings House? In their inner sanctum?

"No. I'm interested," I said.

"Figured as much," Noelle replied.

"Good," Ariana said with a small smile. "Kiran will come get you."

All the tension and fear and anger melted away as I was over-come with hope. They were letting me in. They were finally letting me in.

"Oh. And you can have this back," Ariana said, handing me the test. "I don't even take physics."

Then they sauntered off together, tossing their laughter back at me, as I stood in the middle of the dark campus, unable to so much as breathe.

INSIDE

Anticipation gripped my heart as I followed Kiran up the front walk toward Billings House. I stared up at the windows overhead, giddy as could be. Any moment now, I was going to see what was behind them. Any minute now, I would be privy to the secrets that this place held. I felt like I was being ushered into some secret society. Would I be greeted by girls in white robes and forced to sign some document in blood, swearing I would never repeat what I saw within these walls? Somehow that wouldn't surprise me, especially after last night.

Kiran paused in front of the door and raised one eyebrow. "You ready for this?"

All I could do was nod. She smirked and pushed the door open. This was it.

I followed Kiran into the lobby and tried not to look too awed or intimidated.

"Here we are," she said. "Home sweet home."

"It's nice," I said. Understatement of the year. The Billings foyer was large yet cozy, with high ceilings crisscrossed by wooden beams. A stone fireplace took up one wall and the floor was hardwood, covered by a gorgeous handwoven rug. Framed photographs of Billings girls through the ages adorned the walls. In these photos I recognized a couple of politicians, one famous news anchor, and at least two groundbreaking authors. I would have studied them all more closely if I hadn't thought it would make me look too eager.

Upstairs was all plush carpeting, bronze wall sconces, and artistic photos of the Easton grounds. I could hear music playing through someone's wall. When we walked into the room Taylor and Kiran shared, Taylor was hanging backward off the end of her bed reading one of her romance novels upside down.

"Hi, Reed!" she said, flipping over. She closed her eyes against a head rush, then smiled.

"Do you *ever* study?" I asked her.

"She doesn't have to. She just picks up her A's like she's picking up mail," Kiran said, slinging her bag onto her own bed. "It's so annoying."

Their room was huge. Kiran's bed, covered in a hundred shades of purple in satins and silk, stood near the bay window. Taylor's, covered in red and pink, sat clear on the other side of the room with a dance floor's worth of space in between. They also had their own fireplace, in which stood a dozen white candles of all shapes and sizes. Their desks were twice the size of those in Bradwell, and they had double dressers.

"It's not my fault God gave me a photographic memory," Taylor said. "Do you know what percentage of the population has a photographic memory?" she asked me.

"I kinda doubt she cares." Kiran scoffed as she shrugged out of her velvet jacket. "I was hoping that living with her would make some of it transfer by osmosis, but so far, no luck." She took the pins out of her bun and let her long hair tumble over her shoulders. "Make yourself comfortable. I need to use the facilities."

She walked past Taylor's bed and opened the door to what I had thought was a closet.

"Less than point-zero-five percent," Taylor whispered proudly as soon as Kiran was gone. "Though some scientists maintain that it doesn't actually exist."

"Ah," I said distractedly. I was too busy staring after Kiran. "Is that a *bathroom*?" I whispered.

"I know," Taylor said, folding over the page on her book and tossing it on her desk. "This place is sick. Everyone wants to get in here. It's the best dorm on campus."

Yeah. No kidding. I was about to ask Taylor how exactly one wrangled an invite to Billings, but there was a flush and Kiran reemerged.

"So, you ready to get to work?"

My heart fell. Work? Did they have another task for me? Was that why I was really there?

At that moment the door opened and in walked Noelle and Ariana. I was half pleased, half miserable to see them.

"What? You haven't even started yet?" Noelle asked, raising an eyebrow.

"We were waiting for you," Taylor said.

Okay. This was sounding more and more frightening.

"How thoughtful," Ariana said.

She walked over to a pair of double doors and slid them open.

"Reed Brennan, welcome to your reward," Kiran said.

My eyes widened. The closet was bigger than any I had ever seen, and filled from end to end with lush sweaters, shimmering tops, silky skirts. The shoes alone were enough to send a girl reeling— even a girl who had never been all that big on fashion. Now I wondered if that had been by choice, or if I was actually a closet clothes hound who just never had the money to feed her habit.

"I think you're a summer," Kiran said, finger to chin as she studied her wardrobe. "That means blues, grays, silvers. Oooh. I have an idea." She rubbed her hands together, then dove in, pulling clothes out and hooking the hangers over her fingers. Once she'd gathered half a dozen items, she walked over to her bed and started laying them out.

"She thinks *I'm* a genius; wait till you see her at work," Taylor said quietly. "I always wished I was good with colors, but it's very rare to have both academic and artistic genius. Of course, there was Leonardo DaVinci, Benjamin Franklin—"

"Taylor," Noelle snapped.

Taylor reddened and pressed her lips together.

"What's going on?" I asked.

"We are giving your wardrobe a makeover," Noelle said.

"You have gorgeous features, you know," Kiran said. "You need to learn to play them up."

I flushed as I watched her pull items from her closet. Suddenly this felt a lot like charity. "I've never been big on fashion."

Kiran snorted. "We noticed."

"You don't *have* to take anything," Ariana said, sitting on the end of Kiran's bed. "But just try some things on. You might like them. You never know."

I was touched by their offer even as I felt chagrined by the suggestion that I needed help.

Kiran placed a pair of gray pants below a blue ballet-neck sweater. A silver skirt was topped by a white short-sleeved turtle-neck. She placed a few more outfits, then clucked her tongue and moved it all around.

"Here. Try this," she said, shoving an aqua shell at me with a gray skirt. The fabric of the shell was softer than anything I had ever touched.

"Okay. Be right back," I said, turning toward the bathroom.

"Aw, she's shy," Kiran teased.

"What?" I said.

"Just change," Noelle said, impatiently. "You don't have anything we haven't seen before. At least I hope you don't."

I glanced at Taylor, who smiled encouragingly. Ariana simply stared with those eerie blue eyes. Feeling beyond self-conscious, I laid the clothes over Taylor's desk chair, then unhooked my jeans and stepped out of them. The Billings Girls watched my every move. It wasn't as if I had never changed in front of girls before, but I'd never had four people staring blatantly at me while I did it. I turned my back to them as I pulled off my T-shirt and quickly yanked on the shell. Even in my tense state I couldn't help but notice how amazing the buttery softness felt against my skin. Then I stepped into the skirt, the satin lining swishing coolly up my legs. I fastened it quickly around my waist, covering up my cotton underpants as fast as possible.

I zipped the skirt and turned around, flushed and hot. I lifted my hair out and let it fall down my back. "What do you think?"

Everyone studied me. I tried to remember whether or not I had put deodorant on that morning. How embarrassing would it be if I handed back Kiran's clothes and they were thick with BO?

Ever so slowly, Noelle smiled. "I think there's hope for you yet."

"Go look in the mirror," Ariana said.

I stepped over to the full-length mirror in the corner and grinned at my reflection. It was a totally new Reed. I looked older. I looked like I had curves. I looked *good.*

If I could show up for lunch with Thomas's parents wearing something like this, they might even think that I was good enough for their son.

"I can borrow these?" I said as Kiran stepped over with another outfit.

"Borrow? You can have them," Kiran said.

My jaw dropped. "What?"

"Please. I get new stuff shipped in every week from Milan . . . New York . . . Paris," she said. "It's not like it's a big deal."

"Thank you so much!" I trilled. "This is exactly what I needed!"

"For what?" Ariana asked shrewdly.

I felt something sink inside of me and looked back at my reflection. "For my wardrobe," I answered cagily. "You guys know I have nothing this nice."

"Thus the reason you're here," Noelle said, rolling her eyes. "Let's get on with it already."

Kiran handed me the next outfit, even more amazing than the last, and I hid a pleased smile as I turned my back to the girls once again. Who cared anymore whether they had tricked me into getting that test for no reason? This was worth every last minute of torture. This made *all* of it worthwhile.

A IS THE NEW C

My heart pounded as Mr. Barber handed back our most recent quiz. It was the first test I had taken using Taylor's new study method, and although I had felt like I knew all the answers when I was filling them in, I was still tense. I had to do well on this. Later in the day I'd be getting back more grades, and I felt like whatever I had scored on this one would set the tone for the rest of my classes. If all did not go well, my days were numbered. I thought of Billings and my afternoon with the girls. I thought of Thomas. I thought of all the things I would lose if I had somehow screwed this up.

Then I thought of my mother. Of the gray walls of Croton High. Of the nothingness I would have to go back to.

I could not go back.

I stared at the cover of my notebook as Barber walked up and down the aisles, using every ounce of willpower I had in me not to mark his progress.

And then his shadow fell across my desk. I held my breath.

"Miss Brennan," he said.

I looked up. He was glaring down at the stapled pages in consternation. He flicked his gaze at me.

"Much improved," he said.

My heart leapt as he placed the test face down on my desk. I fumbled with the pages and finally turned it over. There was a big, fat A right next to my name.

"Wow. Go you," Constance said, leaning over.

I beamed, tingling with triumph. This was going to be a very good day.

A DOSE OF REALITY

"I aced it! *All* of it. Taylor, you saved my life."

Taylor's face shone with pride. We were on our way to dinner and a cool wind had kicked up, pulling the first yellow leaves from the trees. It sent Taylor's golden curls dancing around her cheeks. "Really? You aced *all* of it?"

"Well, not art history," I said. "I only got a B on that test. But I still think it was totally unfair."

"But a B is great, Reed! You did it," Taylor said, grabbing me up in a hug.

"Not without you, I couldn't have," I told her, grinning. "I'm so relieved, you have no idea. I mean, after my last meeting with Naylor I really thought I was out of here."

"Have you told Thomas yet?"

My heart thumped. Apparently I hadn't been that great at keeping the depth of my relationship with Thomas a secret. Of course, from the look of excitement on Taylor's face she didn't seem to mind as much as, say, Noelle might have.

"Not yet," I said, my throat dry. "I haven't seen him."

"Well, come on. He's always lurking around the cafeteria before dinner. Let's tell him," Taylor said, grabbing my hand.

I laughed as she pulled me across the quad. I felt weightless and free. I couldn't stop smiling.

Thomas wasn't near the door as he sometimes was, but this didn't deter Taylor. She walked me right around the north side of the building and there he was, surrounded by his usual posse . . .

. . . handing over a small bag containing half a dozen white pills. Taking a crisp, folded bill and slipping it into his pocket.

I stopped in my tracks. The ground tilted beneath me. I broke out into a cold sweat and all of the sudden I understood everything.

Thomas was dealing drugs? Thomas was dealing drugs. Right there in front of me. Right there in front of everyone. This was why he was so popular. So powerful. This was why he was always surrounded by students. They weren't his friends. They were his clients.

"Oh, shit," Thomas said, seeing my face.

I turned around, flinging Taylor's hand from my arm, and ran.

"Reed! Wait!" Thomas shouted. "I'll catch up with you guys later," I heard him add to his clientele.

I flew around the corner and jogged off. Away from the cafeteria. Away from them all. Where I was going, I had no idea. I just had to go.

"Reed!"

Thomas grabbed my arm. I snatched it away.

"What's the big deal?" he said.

I whirled on him. "What's the big deal? Are you kidding me?"

He knew about my mother. Knew she took pills and knew what they did to her. What she did to me. How could he stand there and say this wasn't a big deal?

Taylor hovered behind him, uncertain. She held the fingers of one hand with the fingertips of the other and tried not to stare.

"What?" Thomas said, having the gall to smile. "Someone has to supply this stuff. It's just a way to make some spending money. Chill out."

Like he needed a way to make some spending money. His watch was worth more than my car.

"Okay, Thomas, if it's not a big deal, then why didn't you tell me?" I asked him.

"Maybe because I knew you'd freak out," he said, his expression darkening. "You're so good, Reed. I didn't want you to think I wasn't."

"Well, lying is really going to help your case there," I said. Suddenly I realized this wasn't the only thing he had lied to me about. "Your phone. The cell phone that you lost that you were so worried about. It's not your parents' phone, is it?"

His jaw clenched. "No. It's not."

My heart felt like it was going to beat itself to death. "It's the phone they call you on, right? Your *clients*? And, what? Your suppliers, too? Is that why you were so freaked?"

His face said it all. "They're not the nicest people in the world, Reed. They have to be able to get hold of me."

"God, Thomas. What are you going to tell me next? That all the crap about your parents was made up too?" I asked.

"No. It's not," he said. "Reed, I wouldn't lie to you about that. I wouldn't lie to you about the important stuff."

Because being a drug dealer was not important.

"I have to go." I started to walk again. He grabbed me again. "Let go of me, Thomas."

He stepped around me. Looked into my eyes. Somehow it hurt even more when he did that. He reached for my arms and I let him touch me.

"Reed, come on. You're not mad," he said, his palms cupping my upper arms. His hands were warm. "You're not. You love me, right? If you love me, you have to love everything about me."

I swallowed hard. I had never told him I loved him. He was standing there, in this awful moment, putting important words in my mouth. Throwing them around as a means to an end. How could he do this to me? I had given myself to him. Given him all of me. And he had been lying to me the entire time. Who the hell was this person? "Thomas—"

"What? You're not . . . ," he scoffed, stepping backward. "You're not breaking up with me over this."

I looked at him, feeling desperate. Feeling used and dirty and stupid and wrong. I just wanted to get away from him. I just wanted to get away and think.

"I don't know," I said.

The defiance was gone instantly. I swear I saw fear in his eyes. "Reed, no. Please. You can't leave me. You . . . you love me."

"Thomas—"

"Reed, please," he said.

That almost sucked me in. The begging.

"I . . . I need some time," I told him.

"No," he said, clutching my hand, keeping me in place.

"Thomas, please," I said. "Let me go."

He searched my eyes. I made myself hold steady. Finally he released his grip, pulling both his hands back as if he were under arrest. Then he put them behind his head for a second and bit his lip. He was trying to think of something to say. He looked like he was about to cry. I couldn't take it anymore. I stepped around him and took off for Bradwell.

"Reed! Reed! Where are you going?" Taylor called, running to catch up with me. "Did you know about this?" I demanded, realizing she had known exactly where to find him.

"Well, yeah," Taylor said with a shrug. "He supplies everyone in Billings. How could you not know that?"

I tasted bile in the back of my throat. I was going to be sick. I didn't know anyone. I didn't know anything. I *was* a naive, ridiculous, newbie sophomore.

"Are you okay?" she asked.

"I have to go," I told her. Then I took off, sprinting into the oncoming darkness.

THE LAST STRAW

This time, I was wide awake, obsessing about Thomas, when my cell phone beeped. I had silenced the ringer hours ago after the twentieth angrily pleading message from Thomas, but had neglected to do the same with the text alert. I picked the phone up slowly and stared at the message.

MEET BEHIND BILLINGS. U HAVE 3 MINS.

I lay there for a long moment. I was not in the mood. Not after Thomas. Not after Taylor's blithe dismissal of his dealings. Not now that I knew what I knew. I was in no mood to do anything for anyone. To trust anyone in the slightest. I was in no mood to move.

My pulse raced. I stared at the ceiling. I could ignore them. I could. I was my own person with my own thoughts and feelings. I would be fine.

Except that I wouldn't. If I ignored them, I would have nothing. No Thomas. No Billings. Nothing. If I ignored them, I'd be just another nameless, faceless, struggling sophomore like Constance. I would always be the Reed Brennan who had arrived at this school all awkward and alone and clueless. I had come a long way since then. Could I really go back?

The phone beeped again. I checked the screen.

TWO MINS.

I whipped my covers aside, got dressed, and forced myself to walk at a leisurely pace all the way down the stairs, out the door, and over to the far side of Billings. I was so full of anger that my jaw hurt from clenching it and a headache had started to throb against my temples. Behind Billings, Noelle, Ariana, Kiran, and Taylor all waited. The night was cool, and they were all bundled into lush sweaters and jackets.

"Are we infringing on your time or something?" Noelle asked.

"What do you want?" I said coolly.

"Oh, so we're doing attitude again, then," Kiran said.

"Kiran," Taylor said in a warning tone. Everyone looked at her. Interesting. Scolding was usually Ariana's job. Apparently Taylor was feeling sorry for me after witnessing my breakup and breakdown. Had she not told everyone else about what had happened, or did they just not care?

Noelle stepped forward and looked down her nose at me. "We have another job for you."

I stared back at her in stoic silence.

"You know that Thermos that Mr. Barber is always carrying?" she said.

"Yeah."

What did they want me to do? Steal that, too?

"Before class tomorrow, we want you to spike it with this," Noelle said.

Ariana stepped forward with a bottle of vodka and held it out. I stared at it.

"What? Why?" I said.

"For fun," Kiran said with a shrug. "He'll probably spray the room with it."

"And someone will smell it and report him and there will be an investigation . . ." Noelle said leadingly, tilting her head to the side.

Kiran snickered and Ariana smirked. Taylor looked down at her feet. They had to be kidding me.

"He could get fired," I said.

"Now *that* would be fun," Noelle said. And they all laughed.

My fingers curled into fists. I was already entirely on edge, but this was enough to send me over. They couldn't mess with people's lives like this. Okay, maybe I had let them mess with mine, but that was my decision. And at least everything I'd done for them in the past had benefited them in some way. Running for food, breaking up with guys, keeping Kiran's secrets, stealing tests. . . . Well, except for that. But when they had asked me to do it, it had *ostensibly* been for their benefit. But there was no way I was going to help them get a man fired just for fun. No matter how much of an ass he was.

"No thanks," I said, turning to go.

"What?" Kiran snapped.

"I thought you hated the guy," Noelle said.

I paused and tipped my head back. "So what?" I asked the sky.

"So . . . why not get him booted?" Taylor said.

"He deserves it," Ariana put in. "After what he did to you."

"What he did to me?" I said, turning to face them.

"On the first day of classes," Ariana said, staring through me.

"*How* do you know about that?" I demanded, letting my voice get dangerously loud. Not one of them seemed to notice or care.

"This is a small school," Noelle said. "No one keeps secrets from us."

I begged to differ. There were lots of secrets at this place. It was just that they were all being kept from me. I glanced at Kiran, who struggled not to look away. At least *most* secrets were being kept from me.

"I'm not doing this," I said, backing away toward Bradwell.

"You sure about that?" Noelle asked.

"You do realize what you're giving up," Kiran said, crossing her slim arms over her chest.

I looked up at Billings, my breath making steam clouds in the cool air. I looked at the arched windows through which I had first spied Ariana on that first night. I recalled the longing I had felt. The need. The feeling that these girls could be the ones to save me. Rescue me from a life I never wanted to have.

I wanted it. I wanted it all so much. But a girl had to draw the line somewhere. This was the place.

"I'm not getting a man fired just because you guys feel like it," I told them, looking each and every one of them in the eye, one by one. I could see the doubt in their eyes. The absolute belief that I would cave. It only made my conviction stronger. I was sick of them screwing with me. Of the Billings Girls and Thomas and everyone at this damn school thinking it was perfectly fine to mess with the new girl's head. "There are certain things even I won't do."

My legs shook as I turned away from them. Turned away from the new life I was so close to winning. Turned back into the familiar darkness.

INTRIGUING DUO

Thursday morning in art history class, I stared out the window at the newly fallen leaves that skittered across the grass, as Ms. Treacle droned on. I didn't even care if the old woman called on me about the reading, which I hadn't done. I wasn't even entirely sure where I was.

I had turned the Billings Girls down. I had said no. In the gray light of day, I started to wonder if I was not a little bit insane. What did I think I was going to do here without them? My relationship with Thomas was over. I had ostracized myself from all the girls in my own class. I had thought I was being all moral and admirable. Now I realized that all I had done was effectively demolished my one and only hope.

I would never be a Billings Girl. I would never be anything but poor little Reed Brennan with the blue-collar father and the addict mother. There was no escape.

Suddenly, as if conjured by my thoughts, one of the Billings Girls appeared in my line of sight. Leanne Shore was being led along one of the brick pathways by Mrs. Naylor. Leanne looked nervous and sick, like she was about to pee in her pants. Something was up, and I wasn't the only one who noticed. I heard Missy and Lorna behind me, whispering as we followed the duo's progress.

They turned up the pathway to the administration building and disappeared through the heavy wooden doors. My heart pounded in my ears.

"*Some*body's in *trou*ble," Missy sang under her breath.

There would be no concentrating for the rest of the day.

SECOND CHANCE

By dinner everyone had heard the news. Leanne had been accused of breaking the honor code. The dirt was she had cheated on an English exam. There was going to be an investigation and if she was found to be guilty, she would be expelled. Leanne didn't show her face in the cafeteria that night, which was probably a wise idea, considering all anyone was waiting for was her arrival. I was dying to talk to the Billings Girls about it—to find out what they knew—but they hadn't spoken to me all day. Hadn't even looked in my direction when I passed them by in the quad. Knowing there was no way I could even attempt to sit with them, I had spent both breakfast and lunch in the infirmary and had planned to spend dinner there too, until my aching, empty stomach convinced me otherwise.

I stepped out of the line with my tray and glanced toward the Billings table, where everyone was huddled together whispering. In fact, everyone at every table was huddled together whispering, sharing the latest tidbits of gossip. I took a deep breath and started for Constance's table, knowing that Missy and the others would get on my case for suddenly sitting with them again. It was just another pain I'd have to endure on my elaborate fall from grace.

I was halfway down the aisle when Thomas stood up from the end of a table and blocked my way. My heart flew into my throat. I hadn't even noticed him there. His skin seemed translucent under the pale lights.

"I need to talk to you," he said, his gaze intense.

I glanced right. Noelle and Ariana both looked away. They had been watching.

"Don't look at them. Look at me," Thomas said. He was being particularly loud.

"Thomas—"

"I called you a hundred times last night. Why are you avoiding me?" he asked, turning suddenly petulant.

"I think you know why," I told him.

"Please, Reed. Just give me a chance to apologize," he said. "You owe me at least one chance."

I looked into his pleading eyes and felt myself start to crumble. Whether from the urge to get out of the spotlight or from an actual wish to hear him out, I was unsure. But I slipped into a chair at an empty table and he sat down across from me.

"I'm so sorry," he said. "I should have told you. But I wanted to be with you and I knew that if you knew you'd think I was some huge loser."

I stared at him.

"You're not a loser," I said automatically.

He pushed back and slumped in his chair. "Yes I am. I'm not good enough for you. I know I'm not."

He looked so sad and small and sorry all of a sudden that, even as angry as I was—as disappointed—I felt the need to make him feel better about himself. I felt the need to protect him.

"Don't say that."

"No. It's true," he said. "But I can change, Reed. I can change for you."

A lump welled up in my chest and traveled to my throat. No one had ever made me promises like this before. No one had ever counted me important enough. Not my mother, not anyone. But I was still wary. This person was a drug dealer, after all. A dangerous image was one thing. Actual danger was quite another.

"I want you back," Thomas said, leaning forward and taking my hand. He held it on top of the table and stared at it like it was some kind of lifeline. "I'll do anything to get you back."

"Thomas—"

"You don't have to answer right now," he said, cutting me off. "But I want to talk to you some more. Can we at least keep talking?"

Talking wasn't a promise of anything. It was just talking. And it didn't even mean tonight or tomorrow or next week. It was all appealingly vague. "Sure," I said finally.

His smile brightened the room. "Good. Listen, there's this thing tonight. In the woods. Kind of a way to blow off steam before all the parents get here. Will you come?"

"What kind of thing?"

"Like a party," he said. "We get together whatever alcohol we can find and we all meet up in this clearing—"

"And you supply the drugs . . . ," I said sarcastically.

"No!" he blurted. "Not tonight. I won't. Not if you don't want me to."

I took a deep breath. What was I doing here? Did I really want to get involved in all this? But then, something he had said had intrigued me.

"Who's 'we all'?" I asked.

"Me and the guys and, of course, your little friends over there," he said, tipping his head toward the Billings table. "Like Dash could go anywhere without Noelle stapled to his side."

And then I started to salivate. Okay. Let's think logically about this. An illegal party in the woods with Thomas and the Billings Girls could definitely get me booted right out of this school and back into the cesspool that was my hometown. But then going to this private little party would also give me a chance to corner Noelle and the others, to make them hear me out. And to show them that I wasn't a total loss. If I could get a senior guy to invite me to an illicit party in the woods, that had to be worth something. Even if that senior boy was Thomas Pearson.

I would just have to use this party to my advantage.

I looked into Thomas's hopeful, tired eyes and knew how much it would mean to him if I said yes. Even more important, I knew how much it could mean to me.

"Okay," I said. "I'll go."

INTO THE WOODS

That night I lay in bed in flannel pants and a T-shirt, waiting until eleven o'clock, when I was to sneak out and meet Thomas behind Bradwell. I wondered if I was doing the right thing. What would the Billings Girls do when I crashed their party? Would they be angry? Would they turn me around and send me right back? The possibility made my stomach feel weak, but I had no alternatives.

The moment my digital alarm clock clicked over to eleven, I whipped my sheets off and stuffed my feet into my sneakers. I grabbed my denim jacket and the flashlight from the emergency kit my father had insisted I bring to school. Constance, deep sleeper that she was, didn't even stir as I opened the door and tiptoed out.

Outside, the night air was cool and crisp. There wasn't a sound on campus except for the thousands of crickets that blanketed the grounds. Thomas was nowhere to be seen.

I took a deep breath, held it, then whispered. "Thomas?"

Instantly a figure stepped out of the shadows. I nearly jumped out of my skin. Especially when I registered the awkward movement, the slightly bulky frame. This was not Thomas.

I reached for the door behind me and was about to run, but then the figure stepped into the light and I choked out a relieved sigh. It wasn't some insane-asylum escapee. It was just Josh.

"Hey," he said.

When he smiled, everything relaxed. How could I have thought this person was threatening, with his golden curls and baby face? He wore a long black coat over a hooded gray sweatshirt and jeans.

"You scared the hell out of me," I said. "Where's Thomas?"

"Sorry," Josh said, lifting one shoulder. "Thomas sent me to get you. He wanted to get up to the party early."

Nice. He sent his errand boy to come get me? What kind of maneuver was that from a person who was looking for forgiveness? Apparently he was so eager to drown his sorrows that he couldn't even wait for me.

"We should get going," Josh said. "You ready?"

A lump had formed in my throat.

"Yeah," I said finally.

"Follow me," Josh replied. "And stay close."

Josh whipped up the hood on his gray sweatshirt, crouched low, and took off across the quad. I ducked and did the same, cursing myself for not thinking to wear a hat or hood as well. It made perfect sense. The more one was covered, the less likely one could be picked out of a lineup.

By the time we got to the edge of campus, I was out of breath. Not from the run, but from the certainty that at any second floodlights were going to flick on and the entire faculty and staff would be waiting to arrest us. But nothing happened. The campus was as quiet as a tomb.

"This way," Josh whispered over his shoulder.

We stuck close to the tree line, walking up the hill and then along the end zone of the football field. Right behind the scoreboard, which loomed up against the star-filled sky, Josh hooked a left and cut into the woods. My heart pounded as I followed, and the practical side of me suddenly realized that I was following a strange guy I didn't know into the woods in the dark of night. I wanted to say something to break the silence, to ease my tension, but what?

Hey, Josh? I know you look cute and innocent and all, but are you planning on raping me out here and leaving me for dead? Just curious.

I kept my mouth shut.

We followed a circuitous dirt path deeper into the woods. Every now and then the leaves would rustle overhead, sending my pulse into spasms. Just when I was about to buck caution and ask how much farther we were going to walk, I heard a boy's whoop followed by a round of laughter. One more turn and we were standing in a clearing where a small fire had been lit in a much-used rock pit. Kiran, Ariana, and Taylor sat in a circle on a low, flat rock, drinking from a flask and whispering to each other. A half dozen guys stood around drinking from flasks and beer cans and cracking each other up, along with Noelle, who looked perfectly comfortable among the men. Thomas was, of course, in the center. I caught his eye and was surprised when he didn't come right over. Surprised, but somewhat relieved.

I had other business to attend to.

"Want a beer or something?" Josh asked, touching the small of my back.

"No, thanks," I said.

He smiled and loped off toward the fire. I turned toward Ariana and the others.

"Hi," I said.

They looked up, noticing me for the first time.

"What're you doing here?" Kiran said.

I rolled my shoulders back and steeled myself.

Kiran pushed herself up and faced me. She wore a gorgeous broadcloth coat that skimmed the ground. Elegant even in the middle of the woods.

"I . . . needed to talk to you," I said. I glanced at Thomas over by the fire, hoping he would stay away—give me some time. He laughed at something Gage said, took a swig from his beer, and slung his arm over his friend's shoulder. It was as if I weren't even there.

"What about? Is everything okay?" Ariana asked, ever the mother figure. I was touched that she asked. Perhaps all was not lost.

"Yeah," I said. "I just—"

Over Kiran's shoulder, I saw Thomas drop an empty can on the ground and crush it with his foot. He walked toward us, staggering slightly.

"What?" Taylor asked, turning around just as Thomas arrived.

"Ladies," he said with a smirk. My heart pounded. He was trashed out of his skull. He held out both hands to me and bent his fingers. "Come here."

"We were talking," Ariana said flatly.

"I invited her," Thomas shot back.

He grabbed my hand and pulled. Too hard. I fell into him and he tripped back slightly. I reddened in embarrassment.

"Thomas, can this wait?" I said, glancing at the girls.

"No. It can't," he replied, laughing.

He tugged me across the clearing, dancing me backward until I was leaning against a huge tree. Then he pressed both my shoulders back with his hands and kissed me. He tasted of beer and smelled of ash from the fire.

"You forgive me, right?" he whispered, shoving my shoulders back against the tree so hard that I couldn't move. "You forgive me now."

"Thomas—"

He covered my mouth with his. I struggled, but he pressed against me. Holding me there. His hands moved to my waist. I felt him tug at my shirt. Felt his cool hands against my warm skin. Before I knew what was happening, his palms started to travel up toward my bra. I yanked my face away from him with some effort.

"Thomas, no," I said.

"What?" he said blearily. Then he grinned. "Gimme a break."

He lunged for my neck and started kissing me again, his hands groping.

"Hey, come on." Hot tears sprang to my eyes. "Everyone's watching."

Thomas leered. "I know. I like it."

I glanced toward Noelle, who had joined the others. Taylor

looked sickened. Kiran smirked and took a swig of her drink. Ariana, as always, stared. Noelle just looked disappointed. This was not what was supposed to happen tonight.

Thomas pulled away for one second and that was all the window I needed. "Get off," I said through my teeth. I raised my hands and shoved him as hard as I could.

Thomas staggered back and almost fell, but touched his fingers to the ground and righted himself, teetering back up to his feet. His chest heaved. Anger contorted his features. Silence fell.

Don't. Don't embarrass me. I begged him with my eyes.

"Why did you even come here?" Thomas spat. He was either to angry to care or too drunk to notice my silent plea.

"I—"

"Clearly it wasn't for me," he said.

I automatically looked over at the Billings Girls. Thomas followed my gaze and laughed maniacally. "Oh, of course! How could I have been so stupid!" he announced grandly. "She's here to suck up to you!" he shouted at Noelle. "That's what this is about, right, *new girl*? All you care about is getting in with them. *I wanna be a Billings Girl! I wanna be a Billings Girl! They're my* friends! *They're so nice to me!*" he fake-whined.

I couldn't breathe. He was throwing my own words in my face. Words I spoke to him in private.

"Thomas—," I said. It came out as a pathetic whisper.

"What're you, using me now?" he shouted. Thomas stepped toward me. He was right in my face. "Using *me* to get to *them*?"

I was going to throw up. Or pass out. What was he doing? How could he treat me like this after everything that had happened?

"I—"

"Well, sorry to disappoint you, but I can't be used," he said. "And I no longer want you here." He grabbed my shoulders and I gasped as he turned me around toward the path. "So go."

I stood motionless.

"*Go!*" he shouted.

I stumbled forward, my eyes blurring with tears. And then all of the sudden the ground was rushing up at me. My knee crashed into a sharp rock, and as I grabbed for my leg, I tumbled completely and my temple slammed into the ground. I bit my tongue and tasted blood as every bone in my body jarred. Taylor gasped and I squeezed my eyes shut against a sudden onslaught of dizziness.

Through the confusion I felt Thomas kneel next to me. "Oh, my God. Are you okay?"

I flinched away from him and suddenly Noelle was between us.

"Back off, Thomas," she said firmly.

They were watching. The Billings Girls. They saw all of it. The humiliation was far worse than the pain.

Thomas stood and staggered back a couple steps. He looked pale and shocked. "Are you all right?" Taylor asked, crouching next to me.

I tried to sit up. Thomas had shoved me to the ground. In front of all these people. In front of Noelle and Ariana and Kiran and Taylor. Why had I come here? What had I been thinking? All I had done was solidify my nonfuture.

But then Kiran was there, hooking her arm under mine, and hauling me up with Taylor's help. Blearily, I looked around and saw that the Billings Girls, all of them, had gathered around me to face Thomas. I tried to breathe without choking a sob. Tried to wrap my brain around what was happening.

"Thomas, what the hell is wrong with you?" Ariana demanded.

"Come on! You all saw what happened!" Thomas said. "I just told her to go and she tripped! I didn't even touch her."

Noelle narrowed her eyes at him. That gaze turned on me would have cut me dead. "Dash?" she said.

"I'm on it," her boyfriend replied, snapping to. "Dude. We need to talk," he said, wrapping his thick arm around Thomas's shoulders. He pulled him off toward the trees and my knees almost went out from under me. Luckily, Kiran and Taylor were still supporting me.

Supporting. *Me.*

Ariana stepped into my line of vision. "Are you all right?" she whispered, tucking my hair behind my ear.

"What just happened?" I heard myself say. I stared at the ground. At the rocks, the fire, my favorite jeans ripped at the knee. None of it was in focus, none of it made sense.

"Get the fuck off me!"

I flinched and we all turned around to find Thomas throwing Dash away from him. Dash, about twice Thomas's size, nearly fell into the fire, but caught himself just in time. Thomas turned and stormed off into the woods in the opposite direction from the path. For a moment we all just stood there, stunned into silence.

The Billings Girls never left my side. But even with them rally-
ing around me, I was beyond mortified. I couldn't believe they had
just witnessed all that. Thomas's vehemence, his mocking. The
things he had said about how much I wanted them to like me. *What
they must think of me now* . . . I couldn't even imagine. I had to get
away from them.

"I'm going back," I announced.

Noelle's face grew serious. I averted my gaze, embarrassed.

"No. You're not," Kiran said. "Screw him. Stay and have fun."

"I can't," I said, near breakdown. "I have to go."

I turned around and staggered blindly into the path. I heard
footsteps behind me, and then a voice. "Reed, wait. I'll walk you
back." I turned around. Noelle.

A NEW BEGINNING

"That's it. From now on you are staying away from Thomas Pearson," Noelle said. Her footsteps were heavy and unforgiving as we stomped over the cool grass around the football field. "I don't know why you ever got involved with him. New-girl mistake."

With every step, my bloody knee twinged and I winced, feeling the humiliation and confusion anew. I was emotionally exhausted. Thomas had worn me down.

"He said he wanted to apologize," I told her. "He said he wanted to be good enough for me."

"Odd way of showing it," Ariana said.

I hadn't even noticed her there until she spoke, but now I realized that the two of them flanked me like a security detail. I wanted to say something to make myself look better. To erase Thomas's pathetic illustration of me as some kind of loser who was dying for their approval. But I had a feeling that anything I said would just make it worse.

"Are you okay?" she asked.

"I'm fine," I said, hugging myself. "I just . . . don't get it. What did I do?"

"You didn't do anything," Noelle said, her thick hair bouncing back from her face as we descended the hill toward the dorms, keeping close to the tree line. "He's always been a mean drunk. Takes after his father."

"So you think it was just the alcohol talking?" I asked. My heart actually fluttered with hope.

"Does it really matter?" Ariana asked quietly.

"No, it doesn't," Noelle said firmly.

She was right, of course. I never forgave my mother for all the insanity she spewed when she was on a drunken rampage. Why should I forgive Thomas?

"You do realize that you have to stay away from him now, right?" Noelle said. "The guy is asylum bound if you ask me."

I swallowed hard and nodded. "Yeah. I think Thomas and I are officially over."

"Good," Ariana said.

"You're better off," Noelle added.

I almost smiled at her conviction. "Why are you guys being so nice to me?"

They both looked confused. "We're always nice," Ariana said, in a tone that made me think she actually believed it.

"Don't let it go to your head," Noelle said simply.

"You guys . . . about the other night," I said.

"We're not talking about that now," Noelle said firmly. I decided to keep my mouth shut the rest of the way.

We were just approaching the back of Billings House, which was right behind Bradwell, when we heard the sound of tires crunching over gravel. My heart hit my throat and Noelle yanked me roughly back against the stone wall of Billings. We all stood there, not moving, not breathing, the cold stone radiating chills straight through our clothes and into our bones. The wind rustled the leaves over an unintelligible voice, a muffled shout. Then headlights flashed between buildings and the sound of a car engine faded into the distance. Not until I was enveloped in absolute silence could I find the will to breathe again.

"Who was that?" I asked.

"Who knows?" Noelle said. She didn't sound scared, but irritated that whoever it was had put her out for those thirty seconds. "Reed, listen to me. The good news is that Thomas showed his true colors up there, and now you know," she said, casting her gaze up toward the hill. My heart was still catching up and I could hardly focus. "Do not let him back in, do you understand me? If I see you so much as talking to that jackass . . ."

"I won't," I told her, touched by the depth of her passion. Passion on my behalf. "I promise. I won't."

It was an easy choice to make now, between Thomas and the Billings Girls. Thomas had made it easy. For all his talk about not wanting to see me get hurt at the hands of the Billings Girls, it was he who had done the damage. I wasn't going to let him do it again. No matter how much he begged. This time I would be strong.

"All clear," Ariana said, checking around the side of the building.

"Let's go," Noelle said.

They walked me right past the safety of Billings and through the open quad, where they could have gotten snagged by any number of authority figures, making sure I got to my own dorm okay. We said good-bye and I crept quietly inside and up to the bathroom to clean up my wounded knee. With every wince I recalled Thomas's face and told myself enough was enough. If he ever did beg for my forgiveness again, I just had to remember this pain.

Constance was out cold when I slipped in, but I didn't undress, not wanting to risk waking her up and having to explain where I had been. I stepped out of my shoes and crawled under the covers fully clothed.

There was no chance of me falling asleep. I was too wired. I kept thinking about what Noelle and Ariana had said. How protective they had become. How much they clearly cared. I was back in with the Billings Girls. I still had a hope of a future.

And I had no one but Thomas Pearson and his psychotic temper to thank for it.

AN UNEXPECTED VISIT

I dressed quickly on Friday morning while Constance sang along to her stereo under her breath, bopping around the room as she put on earrings and fluffed her hair. I hadn't slept at all. Not for one minute. I was exhausted, but exhilarated. Today I would be back at the Billings table. Today was a whole new start.

I pulled my pair of backup jeans on gingerly over my injured knee and had just fastened the button fly when there was a knock on the door.

Constance shot me an intrigued look. Mostly, the girls on our floor just walked into one another's rooms with no preamble. She opened the door and froze when she saw Thomas standing there. I knew the feeling. The wind was knocked right out of me.

"Hey," Thomas said to her.

He was wearing the same clothes he'd had on the night before and his eyes were bloodshot and watery.

"Can I come in?" he said to me.

My mouth opened, but nothing came out. Somehow he took that as an invitation.

Constance stepped mutely backward as he entered our room.

"You were just going to breakfast, right?" Thomas said to Constance, leaving no room for question.

"Oh. Uh . . ." Constance shot me a concerned look and I nodded at her to go. Whatever was about to happen, I didn't need her seeing it and reporting it to the entire school. "Okay," she said, snatching up her bag. "I'll see you later," she told me. She closed the door behind her as she fled, probably relieved to be out of the room so that she couldn't be implicated if we were caught. I sank down onto my bed, feeling weak.

"What are you doing here?" I whispered.

I didn't want to be alone with him. I felt trapped and cornered. I glanced at the door and wondered if he would try to stop me if I went to leave. I imagined him grabbing my wrist, holding me here, and stayed where I was.

"Reed, please. Just listen to me," Thomas said, sitting at the end of my bed. I instantly curled into the corner. Thomas hung his head. He got up and sat down on Constance's mattress. "Is this better?" he asked.

I let out a breath. "Slightly."

He hung his head and sighed. "I guess I deserve that."

You guess? You guess?!

He looked up at me, his brown eyes pleading. "I swear to God, Reed, I didn't mean to yell at you like that. I didn't know you were going to trip."

I stared at him. What was I supposed to say to that? *Oh, no problem?*

"I don't know what came over me last night, Reed. I—" He stopped and pushed his hands over his face and up into his hair. As always, it fell right back into place. "Well, that's a lie. I do know what came over me," he said.

I was half rapt with attention, half planning my escape route.

"I . . . I have a problem," Thomas said, clasping his hands together. "With alcohol."

For some reason, this announcement uncoiled some of my muscles.

"Aren't you going to say anything?" he asked.

"What do you want me to say?" I shot back. "Duh?"

Thomas blinked. Score one for Reed. I actually wished Noelle could have heard that one.

"I guess I deserve that, too," he said with a smirk. And for some reason, I couldn't help smirking in return. Slowly, I uncurled my legs and sat Indian style against the wall, watching him. It was amazing how different he was from last night. His body language entirely transformed. Not at all belligerent. He looked like Thomas. Regular Thomas. *My* Thomas.

But he was a drug dealer. A liar. A malicious drunk. I had to remember these things.

"It's in my blood," he continued. "Not that that's an excuse. It's not. I just . . . I know I have to get help. I know that. I mean, Christ, I've been wishing my parents would do it all these years, so what kind of hypocrite would I be if I didn't do it myself?"

"So you're . . . going to rehab?" I asked.

Thomas let out a wry laugh. "I would. I really would. But I can't. Not without my parents finding out. I'm still a minor for another six months," he said, looking me in the eye. "And I can't tell them this. They'll just laugh it off. They'll just tell me to toughen up." My heart went out to him in that moment. He looked so vulnerable. And scared. Like a little kid whose parents had just let him down for the ten millionth time. He wanted help, but he couldn't even go to his parents for it. He must have seen the change in my expression because he moved back over to my bed. I didn't flinch when he reached for my hands. For a moment he stared down at our fingers.

"I know you won't forgive me," he said. "But I need to figure this out and I don't think I can do this without you, Reed," he told me, looking me in the eye now. He swallowed hard. "I . . . I need your help. Please. If you're not with me on this, I don't . . . I don't know what'll happen to me."

A tear spilled over and before I knew it, he was crying. Crying in earnest. He leaned toward me and I found myself reaching out to him. Holding him. Letting him sob against my shoulder. How could I have ever thought I could turn my back on him? He needed help.

"I'm so sorry, Reed. I swear I'd never hurt you," Thomas said. "Please. You've got to believe me."

He looked up at me, his gorgeous eyes rimmed in red. He seemed so helpless. So scared that I wouldn't forgive him, that in that moment I was ashamed. Ashamed for being so disloyal. The way he'd acted toward me—it was an accident. A mistake. Everyone made mistakes. And besides, he loved me. I knew he did. I was all he had.

"Okay," I said quietly, clinging to him. "I'll help you. Whatever you need."

"Thank you," Thomas cried into my sweater.

As his sobs slowly quieted, I sat there and thought of Noelle. I knew what she would do in this situation. She would be strong. She would get up and tell him to go to hell. That she didn't need this kind of crap in her life. But all I wanted was to keep holding him. I wanted both of us to feel that everything was going to be all right.

Eventually Thomas took a deep breath and sat up. He wiped under his eyes and shot me an embarrassed smile. But even with a red nose and a tear-streaked face, he was still beautiful. So incredibly, amazingly beautiful.

"Are you okay?" I asked, my heart heavy.

"I will be. Now." He took another deep breath and blew it out. "Listen. There's . . . one more thing. I know I have no right to ask this, but I'm hoping . . . I'm hoping you'll still have brunch with us tomorrow," he said. "My parents are expecting to meet you and I know they'll love you."

He was right. He didn't have any right to be asking me this. But he was so sincere. So troubled and sad and penitent. He was laying his heart out on the line for me and I didn't have it in me to crush him.

Not even with Noelle's voice ringing in my ears. Telling me that if I ever spoke to him again . . .

"Okay," I said, my throat dry. "I'll be there."

Thomas's whole body relaxed. His grateful smile touched my heart and I knew right then that I would do anything for him. I did love him. Nothing that had happened had changed that. I was in for whatever was coming. The thought both excited and petrified me.

"Thank you," he said, leaning forward to kiss my forehead. I closed my eyes and fought the urge to cry. He kissed me again, on the lips this time, then slipped out.

WALK OF SHAME

When I stepped out the back door of Bradwell alone fifteen minutes later, I was both emotionally and physically exhausted as well as completely unprepared for the sight that met me. A huge crowd of students had formed around Billings and the throng grew with each passing second. What had happened now? My blood pressure raced as I joined the confusion. I quickly found Constance, Diana, and Missy in the crowd.

"What's going on?" I asked.

"Hey, are you all right?" Constance asked me pointedly.

It took me a second to realize she was talking about Thomas's visit. Two seconds of intrigue and I'd forgotten all about him.

"Yeah. I'm fine," I said. "What's up?"

"They're throwing her out. That girl from Billings," Constance told me, her eyes wide.

My insides overturned and for a split second my mind went blank. For some reason the only Billings girls I could picture were Ariana and Noelle. "Who?" I asked.

Missy rolled her eyes. "Leanne Shore. Try to keep up, Brennan."

I ignored her dig as relief washed over me. Of course. Leanne. Why had my brain gone anywhere else? I scanned the crowd for Ariana and the others, wondering where they were—what they thought of all this. I saw no sign of them.

"So, what happened? Did she confess?" Diana asked, standing on her tiptoes in a futile attempt to see over the dozens of kids in front of us.

"No! They found her crib sheets," Constance said sagely. "I heard from one of the girls at *The Chronicle*."

"Idiot wasn't even smart enough to burn the evidence," Missy said with mock sympathy, staring at the front door. "No wonder she had to cheat."

"Do you think Noelle and the others are okay?" Constance asked me. "Do you think they're upset?"

"Why?" I replied.

"Because, they're all dorm-mates," Constance said. "They must be freaking out."

Missy snorted a laugh and, for once, I was right there with her. The last thing any of those girls was doing at this moment was freaking out. Noelle was probably doing a happy little dance somewhere.

"I don't know. I don't think they were that close," I said diplomatically.

A hushed silence fell over crowd as the front doors of the dorm swung open. Constance instantly climbed up on the arm of the stone bench behind us, which was already packed with people, and hauled me up with her. I was appalled at her insatiability, but impressed by her tenacity. Together we balanced there with a perfect bird's-eye view of the proceedings.

Leanne was the first to walk out, followed by two people I assumed to be her parents. Several members of the Easton staff trailed after them, toting bags and boxes. Leanne was as white as a ghost.

"Buh-bye, loser," someone said. Someone who sounded a lot like Noelle. Quickly, I spotted her and the others front and center, and sure enough, Noelle was waving her fingers at Leanne.

A few people in the crowd snickered. Leanne's gait changed ever so slightly and I knew she had heard. This was awful. As much as I couldn't stand the girl myself, I would never have wished this on her or anyone. Why did they have to do this now, with everyone watching? Why wasn't anyone out here dispersing the crowd, sending us off to breakfast?

"They want us to see this," one of the girls on the bench said as if reading my thoughts. "They think that doing this will teach us a lesson or something."

"Well, I know I'm never breaking the honor code," her friend said. "So, well done, Dean Marcus."

Just then there was a commotion at the front of the crowd. I saw Natasha weaving her way toward Noelle, pushing past a number of people along her way. Steam may as well have been shooting out of her ears. I jumped down from the bench and shoved through the throng to join my friends.

"Reed? Where're you going?" Constance shouted.

"I'll be right back," I replied.

Natasha and I arrived at exactly the same time, me behind Taylor, Natasha right up in Noelle's face.

"What the hell is going on, Noelle?" Natasha demanded, out of breath.

"Didn't you hear? Your roommate is going home," Noelle said innocently. "She broke the honor code."

"Like hell she did," Natasha said.

Noelle's eyebrows went up. "I'm shocked at you, Miss Crenshaw! Are you suggesting that the Board of Directors has made a mistake?" she asked. "Because I would think twice about making that accusation if I were you."

"I'm not accusing them. I'm accusing you," Natasha spat.

I glanced at Taylor, but she hadn't noticed me there. What the hell was this about?

"You might want to think twice about that, Natasha," Kiran said, stepping up. Ariana touched her arm and shook her head as if confrontation was just too gauche.

For the first time, I saw uncertainty behind Natasha's eyes. She glanced around at Kiran, Ariana, and Taylor. Then her eyes fell on me and she took me in as one with the others. As if I was part of whatever it was she was sizing up. Then she mustered a disgusted expression and finally—I thought, wisely—retreated.

When she was gone, my mind reeled with questions, but I kept my mouth shut. Soon Leanne was all packed into her car, on her way back to wherever she had come from. Once the onlookers started to disperse, I rallied the courage to ask.

"What was she taking about?" I asked.

Noelle, Ariana, Kiran, and Taylor all turned around and looked at me, their expressions flat.

"Wouldn't you like to know, glass-licker?" Noelle asked.

Kiran smirked. Ariana stared past me. Taylor quickly looked away.

"Wh . . . what?"

I had no idea what else to say. A cold finger of fear slid down my spine.

"I saw Thomas, Reed," Ariana said. "I saw him leaving your dorm this morning."

My heart squeezed down to the size of a rotten peach pit. "He was just—"

"I thought I told you never to talk to him again," Noelle said. "Or was that just another thing you decided you were above doing?"

Oh, God. Oh God Oh God Oh God. So they hadn't forgiven me for the Barber thing. Or they had, but now I'd screwed it all up again.

"I didn't ask him to come over," I blurted. "He just showed up. Noelle, I swear. I didn't even want to talk to him."

"So pathetic," Kiran said. "She can't stay away from him. I told you."

My face burned with the knowledge that they had been discussing me. Talking about me and picking me apart about last night.

"You guys don't understand," I said.

Noelle narrowed her eyes into a look of sheer distaste. I was begging for my life here and she knew it. And she didn't like it.

"I'm bored," Kiran said with a sigh.

"*So* bored," Taylor echoed.

"Ladies?" Noelle said.

"Noelle," I said, overcome with desperation. My entire world was shifting before me. "Ariana, you can't—"

But they ignored me, looking through me like I wasn't even there. Noelle turned, and Ariana, Kiran, and Taylor all fell into ranks around her, moving off toward their upper-level classes. Just like that. Without me.

ALONE

That afternoon, each of my teachers started off with a lecture on not allowing the recent scandal to distract us, but the classrooms were still full of whispers. The instructors spent so much time reprimanding people for gossiping, they didn't seem to notice me staring out the window, wondering where it had all gone wrong. Should I have thrown Thomas out of my room that morning? Probably. But then Ariana still might have seen him leaving and assumed I had spoken to him. Maybe if I could just get one of them—any one of them—alone, I could explain. If they just heard me out and realized that Thomas had cornered me, maybe I could still win them back.

But then, of course, there was the little issue of Thomas himself. I had told him I would help him. I had told him I would be there for him. I couldn't have both him and the Billings Girls—that much had been made perfectly clear. So what was I going to do?

Just to make my solitude more complete, Thomas was MIA for the rest of the day. Normally I would see him in the halls between classes or lounging in the quad before the bell, but he was nowhere to be found. I checked my cell for messages every five minutes, but there was nothing. Even the sight of the blank screen depressed me, almost as much as the words "Glass-licker's Phone," which I hadn't changed because it had started to feel like a personal joke between me and Noelle. Now it just seemed like a *cruel* joke.

Back at Bradwell after dinner, I kept my phone in my front pocket and listened for the ring of the hall phone, but everything was silent. Even the dorm was quieter than usual, with several of my floor-mates having gone out for dinner with their parents. Most of the families were arriving on Saturday for morning services followed by brunch, but some had come early to whisk their little darlings off to one of the quaint, candlelit restaurants in town. One might think this would make me regret my decision to shut my parents out, but it only made me feel more secure. If anything, we would have been chowing down at the Denny's on the highway while my mother made her coffee Irish and berated me for thinking I was better than she was.

With a sigh, I pushed myself up from my bed and sat down on the window ledge. Ariana's room was pitch black. Most of the windows in Billings were. More casualties of parents' weekend. I pulled out my phone and stared at it, feeling desperate. I needed to talk to someone.

I took a deep breath and decided to start at the bottom. I would call Taylor. She was my best shot at a sympathetic ear. And maybe if she was out with her parents, she would be more inclined to be nice to me.

I was grasping at straws.

I hit speed dial four. Noelle had preprogrammed them for me. She was one. Ariana was two. Kiran, three. Taylor, four.

I held my breath as the phone rang once, twice, three times. Then the voice mail picked up. "Hi! You've reached Taylor's phone! Please leave a message!"

I hung up before the beep. Emboldened, I tried Kiran. Another voice mail. "It's Kiran," she said, sounding bored. "If you don't know what to do at the beep, I can't help you."

I hung up. A slight flicker of anger started to grow inside of me. How could they ignore me like this? Had they all made some pact not to pick up if I called? Shaking, I tried Ariana. Her voice mail flicked on instantly. I hung up before the recorded voice had finished uttering its first word and tossed my phone onto Constance's bed, disgusted—with them, yes, but more so with myself.

Screw this.

I got up, grabbed the phone, and was about to dial Noelle when the door flew open, shooting my heart into my throat. Constance bounced in, all flushed.

"Hey! A bunch of us are gonna watch a DVD. Wanna come?" she asked.

No, I want to wallow.

"Thanks anyway," I said. "I have some phone calls to make."

"Come on, Reed. Lorna's whipped out her entire Reese Witherspoon collection and they're already starting to fight over what to watch," Constance rambled.

"I can't," I told her. I itched for her to go away. The longer she stayed, the longer she prevented me from calling Noelle. From begging for my life.

"Come on!" Constance wheedled. "It'll be fun! You can be the deciding vote!"

"I said *no*," I snapped.

Instantly, I regretted it. Constance looked at me as if I'd just slapped her across the face. I may as well have. All she had done since we had arrived here was be bubbly and kind and solicitous. And all I'd done was ignore her.

"Constance—"

"No. It's fine," she said, grabbing a sweater off her bed. "You call your *friends*."

She turned around and, for the first time since I'd known her, slammed the door.

And there I stood, alone in my room, clinging to my silent phone, listening to the laughter and conversation on the other side of the wall.

THE PEARSONS

At seven a.m. on Saturday I arrived at the end of the walk that led to Ketlar House, coiffed like I had never been coiffed before. I wasn't sure if Kiran would still be okay with my wearing her clothes, but I had decided to risk it. In order to get through this day, I needed to be someone other than myself. And in this outfit I felt like a different person. Of course, my heart was still pounding nervously. I was about to meet Thomas's parents, the infamous Lawrence and Trina. How could a girl not be afraid?

It was a gorgeous, crisp, clear autumn morning. All around me guys greeted their parents with handshakes and hugs before leading them off to morning services. I scanned the area for Thomas, but didn't see him. I did, however, spot his parents. They couldn't have been more obvious if their foreheads had been stamped "Pearson." His father stood at the far side of the walk, the cuff of his pristine gray suit riding up each time he checked his Movado. He was the spitting image of Thomas with just a bit more weight and height, and a few wrinkles around the eyes. Thomas's mother sat perched on a stone bench behind him, her face pinched and her dyed red hair pulled back in a chignon. She wore a pinstriped suit and perfect leather heels that matched her perfect leather bag. She looked, in a word, bored.

Thomas was clearly late. I could have killed him for putting me in this awkward situation. I had never been good at introducing myself to people, especially adults. For a few moments, I waited for them to spot me. After all, they knew that I was coming. Thomas must have described me to them. Wasn't it the adult's responsibility to approach the kid?

But the longer I waited, the more the area emptied out and soon I felt so conspicuous I couldn't take it anymore. Thinking of Kiran's easy sophistication, of Noelle's self-assuredness, I plastered a smile across my face and turned to Thomas's dad. Hey, I could still emulate them, even if they hated me.

"Hi! You must be Mr. Pearson," I said, stepping toward him.

He looked me up and down, his brows drawing together. Behind him, his wife rose on unsteady feet. "Yes. And you are?"

"I'm Reed Brennan."

No flicker of recognition. Not even a blink. My underarms prickled with heat.

"Thomas's . . ."

The word caught in my throat. I found that with the infamous Pearsons staring me down, I couldn't choke it out.

"Thomas's what, dear?" Trina said, catching her husband's arm in her grip.

"Thomas's . . . friend," I said finally. *I want out of here. Now.* "He didn't . . . I thought he told you I would be having brunch with you."

His father sighed. "No, he didn't. But then, that's Thomas. I'm not at all surprised."

I couldn't believe this. Thomas had told them all about me. I was the first girlfriend he wanted them to meet. They were excited to meet me. More lies. I stared at the door of Ketlar, willing Thomas to emerge. If he was in there, playing sick, leaving me alone to deal with these people who didn't even know I existed, then he was the biggest coward ever to roam the earth.

But he wouldn't do that to me. He wouldn't. Not after everything. Not after his confession and apology. Something had to be wrong.

I whipped my cell phone out and speed-dialed Thomas. I smiled at his parents, then turned away. It went directly to voice mail and I snapped the phone shut. For the first time, I wished I had the number to his other phone. Anything to get hold of him.

"Where *is* Thomas, dear?" his mother asked, running her eyes over me. I tucked my phone away.

"I don't know. He must be running late," I said. I racked my brain for some kind of excuse. "He . . . uh . . . has this big paper due and I know he stayed up late last night working on it."

"Thomas? Up late studying? That's rich," his father said.

My face burned. I was no good at this. I could barely handle my own parents. At that moment, the chapel bells rang out, signaling the start of morning services. I looked around. The entire quad was deserted.

The tone of the bell reverberated through my bones as I looked up to the high eaves of Ketlar House. I hadn't talked to Thomas in almost twenty-four hours. Hadn't even *seen* him since his visit yesterday morning. Somehow I knew that Thomas wasn't inside those walls, looking out. I knew it in my soul.

"That's it. I'm going in there and dragging him out if I have to," Mr. Pearson said.

I wanted to protest. To say that I'd go. But he had already stormed like a bull halfway up the walk. Mrs. Pearson sighed grandly and I shot her an apologetic smile, which she completely ignored. The longer we stood there alone, the faster my heart pounded. Something was wrong here. Something was very, very wrong.

I half hoped Mr. Pearson would walk out holding Thomas by the scruff of his neck, still wearing his boxers or pajama pants or whatever the hell a guy like him slept in. But seconds later, when Mr. Pearson emerged, he was red with rage and completely alone.

Thomas was gone.

A MESSAGE

During morning services, I sat in chilled silence with Constance and her parents—a very large man with a very large head, and a diminutive woman whom he totally overshadowed. Constance hadn't spoken to me all morning and had vacated the room to go meet her parents before I had even showered. But when I sat down next to her after chapel, she had taken in my outfit and given me an impressed glance. I took this as a good sign. Maybe the damage I had done last night was not irreversible.

While Mr. Talbot continuously leaned over to his daughter and asked questions about the service—at full volume—I spent half the time craning my neck around to see if Thomas had arrived yet. His parents stood in the back of the auditorium, looking sour and grim. Every now and then when I turned, I caught his mother staring me down. As if I was somehow responsible for her son's slight. Each time I caught her eye I blanched and told myself not to look again. But I couldn't stop. I kept looking until the dean's final address.

Thomas never arrived.

When services were over, I dodged through the crowd, trying to catch up with Josh, but the wall of families closed in on me and I lost sight of him and his parents. Soon I found myself walking back to Bradwell alone, contemplating my next move. I had already tried every one of Thomas's phone numbers a dozen times. What else could I do? Break into his room and toss it for clues? Where had he gone? And why hadn't he told me he was going?

When I walked into Bradwell, I saw Constance and her parents waiting for the elevator. The last thing I wanted was to ride up in that claustrophobic space with a larger-than-life man and his could-be-mad-at-me daughter. It might send me over the edge. I turned around and shoved my way into the stairwell, taking the steps two at a time. Maybe Thomas had left a note on my door. Or maybe he was even hanging out in my room.

A girl could hope.

I arrived at our door, all sweaty and out of breath, at the same exact moment as Constance. She was alone. *Thank God.*

"Where are your parents?" I asked, heaving.

"Waiting in the common room," she said. "What's going on? Are you all right? We all saw Thomas's parents at services. Did something happen to him?"

Hell if I know. But apparently my proximity to the newest gossip had erased her memory of last night's slight.

"I'm sure he's fine," I lied.

I pushed open the door to our room and we both stopped in our tracks. My entire half of the room was bare. No books, no posters, no sheets, no pillows, no soccer ball. Nothing.

"What the . . . ?" Constance said.

"Oh, my God," I blurted under my breath. I felt the room start to spin. "Oh, my God."

"Okay, calm down," Constance said, though she sounded anything but calm herself. We stared around at the bare bed, the desk that had been swept clean, the closet with its big empty space near the end. It was all gone. Like I had never even been there. "There has to be a reasonable explanation for this."

"Like what?" I asked.

I felt like I was having a heart attack. First Thomas, now this. How much could one girl handle in one morning?

Constance looked at me and bit her lip. "Your grades have been better, right?"

For a second everything clouded over. "You think they kicked me *out*?"

"No! I don't know!" Constance said desperately. "I just . . . where's all your stuff?"

"I have to go," I said, walking toward the door on shaky legs. I felt like I was in a dream. "I have to go find . . . someone."

Naylor, maybe. The dean? Who the hell did people go to when all their things disappeared from their room? *Had* they kicked me out?

And then it hit me. The Billings Girls. Natasha's accusation. Her insinuation that somehow Noelle had been responsible for Leanne. Had they gotten me expelled somehow? Would they really go that far just because I had forgiven Thomas? *Could* they really go that far?

A huge knot formed in my stomach. I was going to be sick.

My life at Easton was over. My hopes, my dreams, my future. Everything. Gone.

"Do you want me to go with you?" Constance asked.

"No. Stay with your parents," I said, somehow finding lucid thoughts. "I'll . . . I'll be back."

I hope.

I staggered down the hall and rushed down the stairs on weakened knees, nearly upending myself at least three times. Outside, the sun blinded me and I paused for a second, disoriented. Where was I going? I had to talk to someone, but who? How could I possibly fix this?

Just then, my cell phone rang, scaring the life right out of me. My hands quaking, I fumbled the tiny phone out of my pocket and checked the caller ID. Restricted number. I hit the talk button, having no clue who it was or even who I wanted it to be.

"Hello?"

"What're you doing out there all by yourself, glass-licker?"

My heart slammed into my ribcage. I whirled around and looked up at Billings. Heavy curtains were drawn over each and every window save for one. There, in the center pane, was Noelle gazing down at me. She smiled slowly and I felt an overwhelming chill of fear.

"If you want to know where your stuff is, you better get in here. Now."

"*You* have my stuff?" I said.

But the line was already dead. I looked up at the window again and Noelle was still smiling. She lifted her hand and crooked her finger, beckoning me inside. And then, ever so slowly, the curtains fell closed.

WELCOME TO BILLINGS

The moment I stepped into Billings, my first instinct was to run. Fourteen girls stood in the foyer, forming a semicircle with Noelle right at the center. With the curtains drawn, the room was cast in shadow. Candles flickered on the mantle and every other available surface. Each of the girls held a black candle before her with both hands. I paused near the door, uncertain. Was this some kind of sacrificial ritual? Kill the new girl to expunge the shame she has brought upon them?

Noelle stepped forward. She handed me an unlit candle, took my arm in her iron grip, and led me to the center of the room. The girls closed into a tight circle around us, the flickering light contorting their faces.

Run. Get out now. Run and never look back.

Noelle took my hand that held the candle and forced me to hold it up. She tipped her candle toward mine and lit it. My fingers shook as I gripped the taper. My mouth was gummy and sour. Noelle stepped back and faced me. Her eyes were as flat as weathered stone. What were they going to do to me? Why was I here?

"The women of Billings House receive you, Reed Brennan, into our circle," Noelle said.

My pulse raced ahead so fast I felt dizzy and faint. All the colors and faces in the room rushed together and I had to force myself to breathe.

Receive me into their circle? What did that mean? Did that mean . . . ?

I found Kiran in the dim light and her frank gaze solidified me. Next to her Taylor struggled to stifle a grin. That was when I knew for sure.

I was in. At Billings House. Somehow, someway, I had been chosen to live here. Yes, they had taken my things, but they had taken them and brought them here. I wasn't expelled. I was, in fact, even more accepted than I had ever been.

I was now a Billings Girl.

It was happening. It was actually happening. Overcome with glee and relief, I searched the ring of faces for Ariana. My first friend. The one who had brought me in, who had started it all. I wanted to thank her with my eyes. Let her know how much this all meant. I owed it all to her.

But when I found her, she was staring right through me again, just like that first night when I had spotted her through the window at Bradwell. With the shadows from the candlelight dancing across her face, it was difficult to focus. With every moment her features morphed and changed. In her face, I recognized nothing, and my pulse pounded with uncertainty.

It's just Ariana. What's wrong with you?

Noelle stood next to me and faced the others. I stared at Ariana, transfixed, unable to look away. I was desperate for a glimpse of the girl I knew, but there was something wrong there. Something off.

"Ladies?" Noelle said.

"Welcome, Reed! To our circle!" they chorused.

Ariana's flame finally held still and she came into sharp focus. My breath caught. As she looked through me, I saw through her. And all I saw was blackness.

Noelle leaned toward my ear. Her whisper so hushed, it was barely a breath.

"You're one of us now."

With that, the candles died as one and darkness consumed us all.

You're invited to a sneak peek of
the next book in the Private series:

SOMETHING RIGHT

"That's all right," Whittaker replied. "Here. Let me help."

He placed one of his solid arms around me and I instantly felt more secure, less wobbly. I managed to get the top off the flask and took a long drink. Mmmmm. The Hayes special was yummy. And Whittaker was so warm. I closed my eyes, savoring the moment, and tipped the flask back. Once again the spinning. I flinched and the liquid went down the wrong pipe. All airways closed off and I choked, spitting alcohol everywhere.

"Are you all right?" He asked.

"Fine! Fine!" I choked, doubled over. Whittaker fished a handkerchief out of his pocket and handed it to me. I coughed into it and wiped my face. The handkerchief was soft, smelled of musk, and had his initials embroidered into it. Old school all the way. But somehow I was not surprised.

"I'm so sorry," I said, finally catching my breath. I tried to hand the handkerchief back to him, but he closed his hand over mine, which closed over the cloth.

"Keep it. It's yours," he said.

I flushed. "You must think I'm a total loser," I said with a snort.

"Quite the contrary," he said, looking into my eyes. "I think you're extraordinary."

And then he was kissing me. It was fine at first, and even though my mind flashed on Thomas, I kissed him back. In my drunken state I let Noelle's arguments cloud my judgment. Screw Thomas. He *had* left me without so much as a word. And if he was out there partying somewhere, as the guys had suggested, then who knew what—or whom—he was doing. I could kiss whomever I wanted to. And Whittaker was a nice guy. Despite his "quite" this and "extraordinary" that. And references to the sixties. I wanted to kiss him. I did. I really did.

I slipped my hands around Whit's thick neck, mostly for balance, and suddenly he got brave. His mouth moved over mine in a rough, unpracticed, awkward back-and-forth motion, so fast it was as if he was trying to create fire with our lips. I grabbed his face between both my hands to stop the madness and he took it as a sign of enthusiasm. Suddenly his tongue was everywhere, parting my lips and darting between my teeth.

He had no idea what he was doing. I wanted to push him away, but I didn't want to embarrass him. Instead, I let him go and hoped he would either suddenly improve or get winded and stop.

Then his large hand fell right on top of my breast and squeezed. Hard. Like he was juicing an orange.

Just like that, Thomas was back. Right there in front of me. With his sexy smile and his gentle touch and his skin against mine. What the hell was I doing? Who *was* this person who was groping me like I was some kind of CPR doll?

My stomach lurched. I held my breath. Oh God. I was going to throw up. I was going to barf in Walt Whittaker's mouth.

My hands flew up and I shoved him away from me. He was just letting out a confused murmur when I turned around, keeled over, and retched all over the bed of leaves behind the log. My eyes stung, my throat burned, my stomach wrenched in pain. Whittaker stood up and moved away, turning his back to me to give me privacy. Thank God. The last thing I wanted was for the guy I had just kissed to watch me puke all over the place.

And then, finally, it was over.

"Are you all right?" he asked me.

It was like his catchphrase of the evening.

I nodded slowly, too mortified to speak.

"Can I walk you back to Billings?" he asked.

I nodded again. Whittaker held out his hands and helped me up. He wrapped his arm around me as we walked back to the clearing and I leaned into him, mushy as overcooked pasta. Everyone stared at our arrival. I could only imagine what I looked like. For a fleeting moment my unfocused gaze fell on Josh. He looked as grim as death.

"Aw! Look at you two, all couple-y," Noelle said with a knowing smile.

"I'm going to walk her back," Whittaker announced, sounding proud.

"Nice," Dash said under his breath.

"Take care of our girl," Noelle said, patting Whit on the back.

From somewhere deep inside of me, I summoned a trace of a smile. Even in my extraordinary state of quite queasy shame, I felt the warmth of Noelle's approval. I had done something right. And that was always a good thing.

CINDERELLA LIVES

The first thing I recognized was the dirty gutter taste in my dry-as-talc mouth. The second was the blinding pain in my skull. The third was the fact that I was freezing. The fourth was the banging.

The banging. The banging. The incessant banging.

"Wake up, new girl! It's after six! You're never going to get anywhere with this attitude!"

Each bang reverberated in my skull and shot a new stab of pain through my head.

I wrenched my eyes open. Then blinked a couple hundred times against their painful dryness. In front of me was the cream-colored wall of my dorm. Below me was my mattress. Nothing else was right.

"That's right, sleepyhead. Vacation's over! Get your sorry ass out of bed!"

It was Noelle. Noelle was yelling over the banging. I flipped over onto my back, the pain in my head nearly blinding, and looked up. I had to swallow back a sudden influx of bile in my throat. Not just Noelle. Kiran, Taylor, Ariana, Natasha, and four other Billings girls whose names I couldn't remember in my current state of excruciating pain, hovered over me. Kiran pounded a red and black steel drum with the handle end of a pair of scissors. Taylor held a DustBuster with grim determination, her eyes hollow and rimmed with hangover red. Natasha gripped my covers in her hands at the end of my bed—thus the goose bumps and shivers.

"What the hell are you guys doing?" I whimpered, squeezing my eyes closed.

The banging, mercifully, stopped. I pressed both palms into my forehead to keep my brain from hemorrhaging.

"It's chore time, new girl," Noelle said.

My brow screwed up in confusion, sending another shock wave of pain through my temples. "What?"

"You didn't think you were done, did you?" Kiran asked. Her highlighted hair was piled up atop her head, and her dark skin shone against the white silk of her robe as if it had been polished. The girl had imbibed more than anyone last night and yet this morning she looked gorgeous enough to be photographed. "No, no, no, no, no. Why did you think we let you *in* here? Now we have access to you 24/7. And that means that you get to do whatever we ask you to do 24/7. That is how it works, isn't it?" she asked with mock seriousness, looking around at her friends.

"Well, yes. I believe it is," Ariana said, her light Southern accent softening the evilness of her words.

"Here," Taylor said, shoving the DustBuster at me. The hangover had aged her normally chipper self at least ten years. "I haven't done under my bed since I've been here. It's starting to affect my sinuses."

Dumbly, I took the contraption from her and held it against my chest, petrified as to what might happen if I sat up. The detachment of my head from my body seemed likely.

"And when you're done with that you can make all the beds," Noelle said. "And vacuum the halls before breakfast. The real vacuum is in the hall supply closet."

I stared up at them, my temples throbbing. They gazed back at me with impatience.

"You're serious," I croaked.

Noelle scrunched her nose, waving her hand in front of it. "I suggest you Listerine first," she said. "I don't want your toxic breath stinking up my room. Let's go, ladies."

Together, they all traipsed out. Everyone but Natasha, who dropped my sheets on the floor and stepped on them with her bare feet on her way to our shared bathroom. I wanted to get up. I did. But between the pain in my skull, the churning in my belly, and the dryness in my throat, it didn't seem physically possible.

"Oh, and if you don't get it all done before breakfast, you'll be taking a toothbrush to the toilets tonight," Noelle said, pausing by the door. "*Your* toothbrush."

"I'm up!" I said, sitting straight. Instantly the entire room caved in around me, crushing my cranium. I closed my eyes against a new wave of nausea.

"That's my girl," Noelle said.

Then she made a point of slamming the door.